FOREVER & ALWAYS

LUCY SMOKE

Copyright © 2019 Lucy Smoke LLC

All rights reserved.

No part of this book may be reproduced, scanned, or distributed in any printed or electronic form without permission in writing from the author. Please do not participate in or encourage piracy of copyrighted materials in violation of author's rights.

Any trademarks, service marks, product names or names featured are assumed to be the property of their respective owners, and are used only for reference. There is no endorsement, implied or otherwise, if any such terms are used.

Forever & Always is a work of fiction. Any similarities to persons, living or dead, places, events, or locales is purely coincidental. The author holds all rights to this work and it is illegal to reproduce this novel without written expressed consent from the author herself.

Cover Design by Smoking Hot Covers

❀ Created with Vellum

*For all my Aussie friends and readers. Thank you for loving me even though it's from afar.
I'll visit again soon!*

CHAPTER 1

Bellamy

"Can you see anything?" I struggled under Texas' weight as he peeked over the top of the brick wall surrounding the outside of Delilah's country mansion.

"Nothing yet. I don't see the girls. Are you sure they're here?" he replied.

"I thought Harlow said she'd be with the girls all night. Aren't bachelorette parties supposed to be like sleepovers? Painting nails and doing hair?" I pressed down with the soles of my feet until I heaved him up further. "Look again!"

"Whoa!" Texas teetered on my shoulders, one of his sneakers nearly slipping off, but I quickly adjusted and he found his footing, shooting me a dirty look as he gripped the top of the wall. "Watch it," he snapped.

"If you think all women do during bachelorette parties is braid hair and talk about boys, I think you're sorely mistaken." A familiar voice came from the side.

I cursed again, and this time when I moved too fast, there was no chance to readjust. Texas came tumbling down and I fell to my knees as he landed on his back and rear.

"You scared the shit outta me!" I snapped as Grayson came walking around the side of the house with his eyebrows raised.

"What are you doing here?" I demanded.

Texas grunted as he stood up and brushed himself off, shooting me yet another dirty look, but I chose to ignore it as I, too, got off the ground.

He shrugged. "Well, I knew tonight was Harlow's big bachelorette party and when I went looking for you two, knowing that the Wiz Kid wouldn't be able to help himself, you weren't there. Of course, I figured you'd be here."

Texas narrowed his eyes on Grayson as the words slipped through his lips, but instead of saying anything about it directly, he turned around and muttered, "Stupid name," before slapping at his pants legs even harder.

I sighed. "Okay, yes, we were just stopping by to check on Harlow and make sure she's okay."

Grayson's eyes glittered darkly with amusement and he shook his head. "Nice try," he said. "But I doubt that's the case. You wanted to know what she's up to."

I shrugged. Sure, I missed her. She was my fiancée, too, after all. I always missed her and if tonight hadn't been her bachelorette party, I would have been at home, cuddling with her after a nice hot make-out session. I'd really rather be doing that than talking with him in the dirt outside some rich girl's house.

Grayson shook his head and pulled his phone out of his pocket, waving it at me as though that was supposed to tell me something. When I didn't reply and instead just put my hands on my sides and growled at him, he huffed out a breath. "I texted Lizzie," he said. "She's at the *Glass Room*."

"What the fuck is the *Glass Room*?" I demanded even as Texas straightened and whirled around, his eyes wide. I looked at him in confusion. "What?"

"We have to go!" he said sharply, rushing off. I stared after him. *Where the hell did he think he was going? I had the keys!* I turned back to Grayson as he struggled to maintain his composure.

"What's the *Glass Room*?" I repeated.

"It's a strip club," Grayson admitted.

I frowned. "Why would Harlow be at a strip club? She's not into women." I knew that for a fact. Hell, I was pretty sure we all did.

Grayson's smile looked painful as though he were in a silent struggle with himself. "Harlow's at her bachelorette party," Grayson said as though that had any significance on the name of the place. I scoffed and continued to stare at him. Finally, he gave in with a bubble of laughter. "It's a *male* strip club."

My mouth dropped open as though my jaw had come unhinged. *There was no way...Harlow wouldn't...but Lizzie would.* I spun around on my heel and followed the path that Texas had taken.

"I'll meet you there then?" Grayson called after me.

I didn't have time to stop and turn around and punch him. He should have told me that before. Harlow. At a strip club. A *male* strip club. God. I was probably going to go to jail tonight.

CHAPTER 2

Harlow

The *Glass Room* was dark, but the music made it feel even darker. The thick scent of alcohol and body oil permeated the air. One of the men on stage turned on his heel and strode back towards the wall, gyrating his hips as he moved. I turned my head to the side, my lips quirking in amusement as Lizzie shrieked in my ear.

When his hands went to his pants, her shrieks grew louder. "Yes!" she screamed. "Take it off! Take it all off!"

My eyes widened when he took her suggestion and ripped the pants clean off his body, tossing the silky fabric to the side so he could spin back around and go to his knees. Women at the front of the stage screamed just as Lizzie was. They panted and threw money at him as he smiled and winked their way.

"You could go up there," Delilah said, looking at me with a smile. It'd been a while since she and I talked, but apparently, she had kept in touch with the guys—and had become good friends with Marv's sister since I'd met her at Ms. Enders' Etiquette Camp. Delilah was nice and she'd grown a lot since the last time we'd seen each other. Apparently, she was now in a New York fashion design school, though she'd rented a country estate to visit for the summer. I guess being the only bridesmaid/maid of honor kind of left Lizzie feeling a little pressured, so when Delilah offered to help host my bachelorette party— or rather, a girls night out—Lizzie being Lizzie, of course, was more than happy to let her help.

And that's how we'd ended up here. At the *Glass Room*. A strip club. A male strip club. I shook my head. If the guys only knew...

Lizzie looked down at her phone as it lit up. It was hard to tell if she was smiling because of what she saw on stage or what she saw on her screen because the wicked grin never left her face. She put the phone away and looked at me.

"I think Delilah's right," she said.

"Huh?" I stared at the two of them in confusion. "What do you mean?"

"You should be on stage. You're the woman of the hour," Lizzie said. "You're getting married tomorrow!"

"Uh...yeah, I know that. But how does that have anything to do with getting on stage?" I flicked a glance at the pantless man in the gold g-string as he whipped around on the stage, leaving a trail of drooling women after him.

"We think it'd be a great idea," Delilah grinned. "Don't

you remember that questionnaire they asked us to fill out when we signed up for the tickets to this show?"

"This is a strip show," I pointed out. "They didn't have any questionnaires."

Lizzie shook her head, touching my arm. "They did. Delilah bought the tickets and filled it out for us."

"Oh." I blinked. I hadn't necessarily expected a male strip club to give its audience members questionnaires, but as I looked around it was a rather nice club. There were two bars along the sides of the room and the stage that the man in the g-string was dancing on. Then several rows of chairs and a back lounge area with circular couches, where we were. "Okay. What about the questionnaire?"

"One of the questions they asked was why we were coming to the show," Delilah said. "And I put down a bachelorette party."

"Okay..." I still wasn't getting it.

Before Delilah could say anything more, the short woman with a headset that had taken our names down at the front door appeared as if out of nowhere. I jumped, startled.

"Hey there!" she said brightly. "Are you Harlow Hampton?"

"Um..." I looked between Delilah and Lizzie who merely smiled at me. "Yes?"

"Great, please follow me and I'll show you backstage." She turned and headed off.

"Wait, what? Backstage? Why would I go backstage?"

"Just go!" Lizzie hissed, shoving me forward.

I gave her an odd look but followed behind the shorter

woman out of curiosity. Maybe they were going to do a meet and greet thing? I mean, I didn't necessarily care to meet the strippers...erm...dancers...entertainers?—whatever they wanted to be called. I was just here to have a good time. This seemed much safer than going to Vegas, which had been Lizzie's initial suggestion.

"Excuse me." I stopped when the woman stopped. "Can you tell me what—"

Before I could finish my question, she turned abruptly and I had to stop myself from colliding with her. She lifted the clipboard in her hand I hadn't noticed her carrying and marked something off before she pulled the side curtain of the stage to the side and marked something off before the lights outside dimmed and new music began to play. "Okay, we're going to ask you to have a seat, now," she said quickly. "Don't you worry about anything. Let the guy do all the work and enjoy."

"Wait, what?" I jumped as a tall, buff man appeared out of nowhere at my side. Jesus, were they all secret ninjas or what?

"Hello," he said in heavily accented English, though for the life of me I couldn't place his accent. "My name's James."

"Hello," I responded weakly, trying not to let it show that my heart had nearly leapt out of my chest.

"I take you with me now," he said, grabbing ahold of my hand and tugging me out on stage after him.

My muscles all locked up. Terror squeezed me tight. What was happening? When he pushed me down onto a chair in the center of the raised platform in front of a room full of screaming women, I almost peed. Just a little. And then the bass dropped.

"Oh, my God." I couldn't believe what was happening. I watched in awestruck horror as the man who had led me onstage began to dance around me. His hands brushed my arms, his fingers lifting my hair. My eyes were wide. My breathing shallow. What. In. The. Ever-loving. Fuck.

A peel of laughter erupted from beyond the crowd, and I had to give the man credit, he didn't fucking miss a beat. But I did. Oh boy, did I. I narrowed my gaze out there into the dark as the lights came up. Lizzie was practically sprawling—standing up—throwing herself on Delilah in hilarity. Delilah, who, for her part in my humiliation, seemed rather amused herself. Lizzie was dying of laughter. Her eyes were squeezed closed, but even from my position on stage, I could see the tears running tracks down her cheeks.

That was okay. It was probably better for her if she died of laughter; because if she was still alive by the time I got off this stage, I was going to murder her. Slowly.

My cheeks flamed red and I squeezed my eyes shut as the man suddenly came to a stop in front of me and—just like the man before—ripped his pants away. There were moans in the audience.

"Oh, geez." I stared in both a kind of awe and just plain dismay as the man rotated his hips in front of me before dropping to the floor and doing a series of confusing gyrating moves that I was sure meant that he had a few extra joints. I was watching with concentration as he moved up to my body, spread my legs and began to give me a lap dance.

I blinked and nearly jerked away, but my back hit the chair and stopped any further movement. I raised my gaze and met a pair of ridiculously amused and also somewhat confused ocean blue eyes across the room.

I gasped out. "Oh. Fuck."

CHAPTER 3

Grayson

When we walked into the *Glass Room*, I don't know what I expected, but it certainly wasn't Harlow on stage with a half-naked male stripper grinding on her. Not half-naked, I amended, damn near-nude. He ripped his pants away, leaving his ass-cheeks on display. If I had to bet, I'd definitely say that his dick was likely covered by a small rectangle of fabric.

Above the crowd, I watched as her head turned and her gaze widened when they locked on me. I met her eyes in a flash of half-confused amusement. I couldn't perceive what my own emotions were telling me. Her look was complete and utter mortification.

Texas bumped against me and stepped back, looking up as he rubbed his nose. "What the hell, man?"

"Take Bellamy somewhere else," I ordered him.

"What?" Bellamy was still at the front arguing with the ticket person, trying to determine if Harlow had even come here. According to what Texas had been saying as we entered—before I got so distracted—he still didn't quite believe it. I grabbed his arm and turned, pointing him to the stage. Texas' eyes widened. "Holy fu—"

"We can't let Bell see," I said. "He'll cause a scene."

Texas nodded. "I'll tell him I thought I saw her walk out with the girls or something. Maybe we can check another part of the club. It's a multi-leveled building..."

"I don't care," I said with a shake of my head. "Do what you have to do."

With that, I left him alone to deal with Bell as I headed backstage. There was a short little woman in black pants and a blouse scribbling on her clipboard while she barked orders into the headset attached to the top of her skull.

"Excuse me," I began as I headed for her, "I have to—"

"Oh, thank goodness you're here," she said. "Where's your costume?"

"My what?" I blinked, drawing up short. I stared down at her as she clucked her tongue at me.

"I guess that doesn't matter. Thanks for coming in on short notice—Joseph had to go. Kept throwing up. Anyway. You have the right underwear on, right? I told Damon to tell you—oh, I'm sure you do. You're a professional. Hurry up and get on stage. Make that girl's night!" She turned me around and shoved me out through the side curtains and just like that, a spotlight fell on my shocked face.

Harlow damn near choked when she saw I had moved from the floor to the stage and the man now gyrating in her face turned, spotted me, and gave me a small, barely discernible nod as he swerved to the side—bending and dancing as he moved around her.

"What are you doing?" the woman behind me hissed. "Go!" I felt a sharp jab in my spine and stumbled forward.

I heard Harlow's groan of dismay more than saw it, but when I looked back to her, she had her face covered with both of her hands. I hesitated still, but with the crowd of women looking on and the spotlight heating my back, I gave in and sauntered forward. If she wanted to have a strip show for her bachelorette party, I guess I'd give her one she'd never forget.

CHAPTER 4

Harlow

*O*f all the things in the world to happen during a bachelorette party, this had to happen to me, I thought, covering my burning face with my hands. *What the hell was he even doing here?* Were the others with him? I thought I'd seen Texas in the crowd, but he'd disappeared so fast that I couldn't be sure.

Fingers trailed down my arm, making me jerk my hands down and Grayson's face appeared before me. "W-what—" I started to blurt out, but he stopped me with a hand over my lips as he tugged me up from the chair. A hush settled over the crowd as Grayson pulled me against his body. I stiffened for a moment before melting into his embrace as he swung me away from the crowd, putting my back to him. His hands trailed down my spine making shivers erupt as they chased after the places he touched.

"Shhhh," he hushed me, his mouth pressed to my temple, warm breath sliding over the top of my ear. A full body shudder worked its way through me. "Trust me," he whispered.

The music changed to a song I recognized but hadn't heard in years. "Ride" by SoMo slithered through the club and Grayson urged me to move against him, his hips pressing into mine, mine into his. The sway of his hips was synced with the music. Heat infused more than just my cheeks, sliding down through the rest of my body. I was hyper-aware of all the eyes on us. He shook his head against me, standing back and leaving me feeling bereft without him there. The other dancer seemed to disappear because, as I glanced around, I realized we were the only two left on stage.

Grayson whipped off his shirt and a few sighs in the crowd turned into delirious moans. I almost turned around and shot the women behind me a glare. He was mine. Before I could, though, Grayson moved back against me. "Don't think about them," he said. "Forget where we are. Dance with me?"

I glanced up at him through my lashes and took his hand when he held it out to me. Though he wasn't a real stripper, there was no denying that he looked as attractive as one. His muscles glistened under the glowing ethereal lights centered on the stage. Grayson's hands grasped my waist and he pulled me forward suddenly so that I fell against him. I heard some twitters from the crowd, but shook my head, shoving them out of my mind.

I let Grayson take the lead, moving me around him as he slid those muscles over me. He gyrated a bit, pushing himself against me and I giggled—feeling ridiculous and a little bit giddy. His arms tensing as he picked me up and sat me back on the chair. My eyes went round as his fingers moved to the placket of his jeans and popped the button. I shook my head furiously and he smiled, a wicked grin that deepened the corners of his mouth. He leaned forward and captured my mouth.

I froze as his lips moved over mine in a familiar way. It was familiar to me. I'd lost count of how many times Grayson had kissed me, but somehow it never got old. My mind went blank as I leaned up against him, forgetting where we were, forgetting about the club and the crowd and the stage. I pressed my breasts to his front and wrapped my arms around his neck and let the kiss take over and consume me.

The music was drawing to an end, the song coming to a fever pitch and then descending. I couldn't be sure if Grayson was still moving or not. He was blocking my sight of the rest of the room, but the curtains were closed, blocking off the back half of the stage from the rest. The screams of the women grew louder once more as the song changed. I assumed that more dancers—real dancers—had gone out to keep them entertained. I didn't care. I wanted to spend the rest of the night in Grayson's arms. I wanted him to keep kissing me until I couldn't remember what it was like *not* to kiss him.

"Oh my goodness! I am so sorry!" A short woman in all black approached us with a horrified gasp. Grayson pulled his mouth away from mine and I whimpered, causing him to flash me another one of his devastating grins as he cupped the back of my head and pressed it against his chest. I inhaled against the slightly sweat-dampened skin. "I didn't realize you weren't one of our dancers, I'm sorry for the mistake. You, of course, will be compensated and, miss, we'll have your tickets refunded immediately."

"Don't worry about it," Grayson said lightly as he helped me to my feet and bent to pick up his discarded shirt.

"But I'm sure we could—I mean after all that you've gone through—I know it's not—" she stumbled through more apologies, her face red with shame and guilt.

Much to my displeasure at seeing all of his flesh covered, Grayson tugged the shirt on over his head. "You've nothing to worry about, this will be a bachelorette party to remember," he laughed.

The woman's eyes went round as she looked from him to me. "Oh my goodness..." she breathed like a frightened bull, her nostrils flaring wider with each inhale and exhale.

I put my hand up to ward off more of her fumbled apologies, but before I could assure her myself, Grayson pulled me closer. "Like I said," he repeated, "there's nothing to worry about. No harm was done. I think my fiancé is more than happy with how the night turned out, isn't that right, Babydoll?" I elbowed him in the gut as a fresh wave of warmth crept over my cheeks. Instead of being angry, though, he merely laughed again and urged me off the stage. "I think we'll call it a night, however," he called over his shoulder. "Thanks for the dance."

I let Grayson lead me out from behind the curtains and through the backstage area. I didn't know how he knew where to go and I didn't ask. I was still half-under the spell he had woven on stage. The way his chest had shone under the lights, the quiet strength of his dancing movements. I felt heat pooling in my stomach. I wanted to shove him into the nearest alcove and jump his bones.

"Grayson." His hand found mine as I spoke his name, but still, he didn't look back. He pulled me through the dark, moving faster than my legs could keep up until I had to half-run just to keep pace with him. "The girls—"

"I texted Lizzie when I got here to let her know you wouldn't need a ride back," he said sharply.

I blinked at the rasp of his voice. He'd sounded so at ease with the woman, but as we moved through the backstage, his steps grew more firm, and on more than one occasion, I saw someone move to stop us. Whatever expression he had on his face, though—that I couldn't see—made them think twice and we weren't interrupted as he yanked me along until we slammed out of an exit stairwell door, the red sign glowing in the darkness.

I squinted as the lighting of the stairwell nearly blinded me. After residing in near darkness for the past hour or so, even the dim fluorescent bulbs made my eyes water. I didn't have a chance to say anything though or ask him to slow down because in the next breath, Grayson dropped my hand and whirled around, pressing me back against the wall as his mouth came back down on mine.

I gasped and he took the opportunity to slide his tongue inside as his hands found my sides and he urged one leg up to hitch over his hip. That wasn't enough for me. Sliding my hands around the back of his neck, I clenched my muscles and jumped. With a quiet oomph, Grayson caught me and slapped a hand out against the wall as his other hand went under my ass as he leveraged me between his chest and the solid white brick at my spine.

"Baby..."

I kissed him to silence any unwanted protests. I'm sure he hadn't meant to take this further than a heated make-out session, but after what he'd just pulled on stage—having to watch the way his hips had gyrated and moved... Well, suffice it to say, the actual dancers hadn't done *anything* for me the way he had.

I nipped at his lower lip as I claimed his mouth, eliciting a groan from deep within his throat. And when I felt the rough fabric of his jeans brushing against the soft skin of my inner thigh, I had never been more thankful for Lizzie's pushiness in all my life.

Dresses are for going out, she had said. *You have to wear one.*

I fumbled as I reached down trying to find his button, but my hand made contact with smooth skin and I realized he hadn't had a chance to button up his jeans. They stayed up around his hips but the front sagged slightly open, covered by the soft cotton of his t-shirt.

"Thank God," I mumbled, tearing my mouth away from his at once as I slid a hand beneath the elastic waistband of his boxers and heard the telltale sound of his rough intake of air.

"No, Jesus, God, no, Harlow." He moved to let me down, but I squeezed my legs tighter.

"Yes," I urged, letting my hand grip the length of him and start to stroke.

"Fuck." He hissed out another breath as I pumped, my

fingers squeezing him relentlessly. "You're going to be the death of me," he said.

I laughed, the sound echoing in the cavern of the stairwell. "I will be," I assured him, "if you don't give me what I want."

Grayson pulled back slightly—just enough so that he could truly look at me without being too close. My eyes met his and I saw the glitter of love in them. It made me bite my lips. "I'll always give you what you want, Babydoll," he said, keeping his voice low as he lifted his hand from the wall and let his fingers trail down my cheek to my neck.

I shivered and shook my head. "Not always," I persisted.

He lifted a brow. "Whenever it doesn't put you in danger," he clarified.

I rolled my eyes but couldn't stop the grin that shone through my faux-irritated expression. Grayson dipped his head and I tipped mine back, meeting him halfway. This time when our lips melded together, it was more than a ravaging need. It went far deeper. I moved my hand inside his pants to the waistband of his boxers once more and pulled them lower, squirming as he kissed me to get his jeans down as well. He broke off with a chuckle.

"Fine, *fine*," he said quickly. "You win."

"Hurry," I said, wiggling in his grasp. The heat he'd stoked inside was about to boil over and I wanted him to be inside me before it did.

Withdrawing a condom from the wallet he kept in his back pocket, he tossed the leather folds to the side as he put plastic to his teeth and tore the side. My eyes widened with the intensity in his gaze as he slid it on and lifted me up higher, reaching beneath the skirt of my dress to feel for my underwear. Putting the fabric to the side—I silently thanked Lizzie once more for talking me into wearing one of those stretchy thongs—he settled the head of his cock at my entrance.

I shifted my hips, waiting, but still, he held there. I grunted in frustration. "What are you doing?" I snapped. I could feel the warmth of him against me, but not where I most wanted it.

His teeth flashed as he smiled at me. "I just like seeing you squirm in my arms," he said just before shoving in all the way to the hilt.

I gasped, my back arched away from the wall. A moan bubbled up out from between my lips. After a moment, I started to urge him on with my hips and he responded accordingly. Grayson pulled back and powered forth. Thrusting in and out of me slowly at first, he began to gain traction.

"Grayson..." I wrapped my arms around him and squeezed my thighs as he slid in once again. His muscles clenched. I felt like a bowstring strung too tightly. I gasped and moaned, my lips pressed to his ear. I could tell every sound I made drove him further and further from rational thinking. He lifted me higher, the strength of his arms making the veins bulge as they rarely did as he leaned his head down until his forehead pressed against my shoulder and he thrust harder.

A moment later—without even lifting his head or breaking stride, his fingers found my hips and canted my lower half slightly up until I could feel the brush of something against my clit. I gasped out and this time, I didn't stop. I continued to get louder and louder as he pushed me into the wall. The warm boiling heat I had felt before grew larger until it became a volcanic explosion and on an inward thrust, it erupted. I cried out, my skin pulled taut as I threw my head back.

I knew even before it connected that I was about to brain myself against the wall, but the pleasure was too great. I couldn't control my movements any more than I could stop the tunneling wave of euphoria that was already sliding through my veins. Almost as if he had expected the movement, however, one of Grayson's hands shot up from my hips and clasped the back of my skull. Then with the same stiffening, he stilled and shuddered against me.

We stayed like that for a while afterwards, until a sharp, jarring ringing noise startled us. He groaned as he let me slide my feet back to the floor. Reaching into his back pocket, he withdrew his phone and sighed, handing the phone to me. "Answer it," he said, removing the condom and tying it off. I watched as he straightened his clothes and moved back towards the door. "And don't move, I'll be right back," he called over his shoulder.

I turned back to the phone and clicked the green button when I saw who was calling. "Hello?"

"Harlow? Where are you? Where's Grayson?" Bellamy's voice came clear through the speaker as I bent down and retrieved Grayson's discarded wallet. As I picked it up, a card slid from one of the folds.

"He's throwing something away. Why?" I picked up the card and turned it over with a frown. There was no symbol or anything. Just a business name and a phone number. I wondered where it had come from.

"Tex and I are waiting outside," Bellamy said. "I can't believe Lizzie took you to a strip club—actually, yes, I can." I could picture him shaking his head with confused horror.

I tucked the card back into Grayson's wallet, resolving to ask him about it later. "We'll be right out—"

"Hey, give me the phone! Spider-Monkey? Where are you?"

I laughed as I heard Texas wrestling the phone away from Bellamy on the other end. "We'll be right out," I said by way of answering as the door behind me opened and Grayson appeared once more.

"We're in parking lot B," Texas said. "In the—"

Grayson took the phone from my hand. "I rode here with you," he snapped. "I know where you're damn well parked."

"Well, Harlow doesn't!" Even though his voice came through a quiet phone speaker, it reverberated in the enclosed space of the stairwell.

Grayson rolled his eyes, his free hand going to the small of my back as he urged me towards the stairs and down them. I reached down and adjusted my skirt and panties as delicately as possible and he shot me a pleased grin that didn't quite match the caustic tone he spoke to Texas with. "She's with me, dumbass. We'll be there in five." He ended the call and swung his arm over my shoulders.

"Brothers," I said lightly. "Can't live with them, can't kill them and bury them in the backyard."

Tossing his head back on a laugh, Grayson readily agreed. "It's a damn good thing they're not blood related to me," he said. "Or else I'd be worried for my mental health."

"Tomorrow, you're going to get married. Believe me," I said, "you should already be worried about your mental health."

His eyes glittered with amusement. "Babydoll, it's been a damn long time coming. A year and a half was about as much as the rest of us could take. Any longer of an engagement and I'm pretty sure Texas would have convinced us to kidnap you and elope to Vegas. Please tell me you'll actually show up to the altar."

Warm summer air filtered over my shoulders as we exited the building. "Guess you'll just have to wait and find out tomorrow, huh?" I said laughing.

CHAPTER 5

"Are you ready?" Lizzie popped her bright fuchsia colored head into the dressing room. Just beneath the top layer of eye-burning pink was an underlayer of soft sky blue. The underlayer matched her bridesmaid dress almost perfectly.

I looked down at the white lace covering my legs and torso. "As ready as I'll ever be," I shot back with a wry grin.

Lizzie took one look at my face and stepped into the room, closing the door behind her. "You're not getting cold feet, are you?"

I shook my head. "No, of course not. I'm just..." I glanced up at the mirror, taking in my reflection. I didn't even recognize myself. The makeup. The hair. The big fucking rock on my finger. It all felt so surreal. Lizzie bounded up behind me, her brightly colored hair popping up at my side in the reflection.

"You're just what?" she asked.

I shrugged. "Ready to get all of the pomp and circumstance out of the way. I wish we were already on our way to Key West."

She made a face. "Why you'd want to go to Key West instead of one of the many countries Marv and Grayson suggested, I'll never understand. Who gives up Ireland?" she asked. "It's Ireland!"

I put my bouquet on the cushioned stool beside me and chuckled lightly. "Where we go isn't important," I replied.

"No, of course not. It's not where you go, it's *who* you go with." She shook her head in mock disgust. "I can't stand how fucking happy the lot of you are. It's sickening. I'm gonna need my prince or princess charming to arrive for me sooner rather than later or I fear you'll turn me into a bitter old woman."

My mouth popped open on an unexpected laugh. "You're barely twenty," I reminded her.

She pouted. "Which makes you having champagne at your wedding all the worse," she muttered. "I can't even indulge. There are adultier adults present. The shame if I were to get shmammered in front of them."

"It wasn't my idea," I said. "It was—"

"Marvs," she said with me at the same time. We paused for a moment, staring at each other in the reflection of the mirror before we burst out in giggles.

"Stop," I gasped as I put a hand to my stomach. "This dress is too tight—I can't breathe!"

"You stop!" she replied just as quickly. A knock on the door interrupted our girlish enjoyment and I half turned towards it, wiping tears from beneath my eyes. Before I could reach for the handle, Lizzie stepped in front of me and shot me a look of faux outrage. "Don't you dare," she hissed. "It's probably one of them and I'm not letting them see you in that dress before the ceremony."

I put my hands up in defeat and nodded for her to go forward. Eyeing me with suspicion, she reached for the handle and cracked the door just a bit to see who was on the other side.

The deep baritone of Knix filtered through the negligent space she allowed. "Is she ready?" he asked.

Pursing her lips, Lizzie looked back at me and I shrugged with a nod. Sighing, she turned back to one of my soon-to-be husbands. "Yes, she's ready. We'll be out there in five minutes." He said something else, lowering his voice so that I couldn't hear and it made Lizzie's lips twitch in amusement. "I'm sure you and the guys can wait another five minutes," she replied. "You'll have a friggin' lifetime after that."

"Tell her I love her," he said, louder this time.

I smiled, a flush stealing across my cheeks.

"She knows," Lizzie replied tartly, snapping the door closed.

I chuckled again and reached for the bouquet I'd set aside earlier. I turned back to the mirror and smoothed out the fabric of my dress as Lizzie approached from behind. "I'm ready," I said, feeling more confident than I had a moment before.

"Moment of truth," she replied. "I hope you are because otherwise, it might be a little difficult to get away. I'm pretty sure Marv is waiting to walk you down the aisle and he'll catch you before you can make it to the front door of the church."

I shook my head at her irreverence. "Let's go."

The doors opened and I held my breath for a moment as a pair of gunmetal gray eyes met mine. Marv held out his arm and I moved forward reaching for it.

"You look beautiful, Sunshine," he whispered as Lizzie took her place in front of us. The wedding march began and she looked back once before starting forward. Through the French door windows that had been pulled to the side, I watched as people I'd come to know so well over the last few years stood in preparation.

I reached up and fingered the lavender colored tie Marv wore, frowning when I noticed a scratch on the side of his neck. I touched it lightly and sent a questioning glance up. Grinning, he took my hand in one of his and brought it to his lips. "Cleo," he murmured.

It was impossible to resist a smile. "I'm sorry," I said.

A smile spread his lips. "You can make it up to me later," he offered lightly.

"How much later?" I asked.

"Whenever you want, Sunshine," he replied. "We've got the rest of our lives."

My heart thudded rapidly against the inside of my ribcage. "Promise?"

He leaned down and brushed a soft kiss against my lips as Lizzie made it to the end of the aisle and moved to stand on one side of the altar. "I'll give you a hundred promises," Marv said against the skin of my lips. "And I'll keep every single one of them."

The returning smile I offered him was something I didn't know I was even capable of. Two and a half years ago, if anyone had asked me where I would be now, I wouldn't have even considered in my wildest fantasies. But the thing about fantasies was that they belonged in dreams and reality was so much better.

~

The wedding was far more than I had ever anticipated. The flowers. The dress. The grooms. Almost as soon as the vows were said and Knix's lips were pressed to mine, I was whisked away into a limo—where Bellamy, Marv, Grayson, and Texas joined us. Texas went straight for the bottle of champagne waiting in a small container of ice. I laughed and screamed as he aimed it at Bellamy's head and popped the cork. The small stopper flew somewhere else, though, landing innocently on one of the empty cushions as Grayson grinned and stole the bottle away, he and Marv filling glasses and passing them around.

"I thought we should have our own little toast," Knix said with a smile, "before we get to the reception venue and have to act appropriately again."

"Acting appropriately is for the fishes," Texas claimed wisely.

I smiled, leaning over and pressing a kiss to his cheek, which he then took advantage of, grabbing me closer with one hand and turning his head as he slid his tongue inside my mouth. I gasped and nearly dropped my glass of champagne, but he quickly drew back with a rueful grin.

"You're terrible," I complained without heat.

"I know, Spider-Monkey." He turned back to the rest of the group and raised his glass. "To what then?" he asked

Knix. "I think we've got everything we could've ever hoped for." He squeezed me closer as if to demonstrate his point.

Knix nodded in agreement, but it was Bellamy that spoke up. "To the most unconventional family we could've ever hoped for," he said, lifting his glass.

The rest of us raised our flutes as well and sipped as the limo traversed the streets of Charleston. A warm glow resided in my chest, spreading outward, crawling across even the most minuscule of cold spots and burning them away.

The only thing that disrupted it was Knix's next words as he turned apologetically to me. "Harlow, do you mind if we put off the honeymoon for another week or so?"

"Why?" I asked. "What's wrong?" He flicked a glance at Grayson and then Marv. "I don't mind." I continued. "But if it's something I can help with..." I let the offer trail off, raising my brows at them meaningfully.

He sighed and then nodded. "Alex asked us for a favor and he knows how important this is to us, so—"

"—for him to ask it must be a big deal," I finished.

Knix's lips pressed into a hard line before a twitching smile appeared. "You're far too smart for us," he said.

I shrugged. "That never stopped any of you before."

Texas barked a laugh and tightened his hold as he downed the rest of his drink and handed the empty flute to Bellamy. "She's right," he said.

"Tell me what's going on," I demanded. "And does it have anything to do with the business card you were carrying around in your wallet?" I asked, turning the question to Grayson.

He blinked as if surprised before he nodded mutely. "How did you—" He stopped and shook his head. "Never mind, it doesn't matter, but yes. Clarissa's niece, Jenna, is working for a law firm in Sydney—"

"Sydney?" I repeated, confused.

He nodded. "Australia," he answered, "and I ran into her boss at the business convention Marv and I went to last weekend. It's his card."

"What was he doing there?" I asked.

"Well, he was actually there because the law firm's original headquarters is stationed in Houston, Texas. The firm in Sydney is a branch. He was visiting and he and a few of the executives were having lunch in the same hotel as the convention."

"Okay..." I eyed them. "What does this have to do with Clarissa's niece?"

Shifting on the seat, he handed his drink off to Marv after barely having more than just a sip. Sitting forward, Grayson rested his forearms on the tops of his thighs as he regarded me seriously. "It appears Jenna has been helping her bosses on a new case that involves corporate embezzlement. She was flown to Sydney a few weeks ago to assist the lawyers in charge of the prosecution. We spoke with Clarissa and she mentioned that the man accused was threatening her niece because she had apparently been the one to find some solid evidence that may very well lead to his imprisonment. Clarissa knew we'd be in town the same time as her boss and she asked us to meet with him on behalf of her niece."

"How would he know it's her?" I asked, confused. To

my knowledge, that kind of information was kept confidential.

Marv answered this time with a frown marring his features. "We're not sure how he found out, but he did and he's left her several disturbing phone calls. We were going to go after we returned from the honeymoon, but two days ago, Clarissa called her and she didn't answer. That wouldn't be much to go on, but Alex says he doesn't feel right. The man Jenna's bosses are prosecuting is fairly powerful because of his business contacts. He's very wealthy and if Jenna were unable to make it to the trial, they'd lose a lot of the information she has. They're worried for her safety, but Alex can't just leave all of his businesses without notice. Knix has a manager to oversee his employees and the rest of us can work from anywhere if need be."

"We should go immediately, then," I suggested. "After the reception."

"I think we can head out tomorrow morning," Knix agreed. "If you'd be okay with it."

I rolled my eyes and leaned over to pop his side as I stared up and up some more—God, was he tall, even sitting down. "I wouldn't have offered if I wasn't okay with it," I said, softening the chastisement with a grin of my own.

His lips didn't smile back. Instead, the corners of his mouth edged downward. "I'm sorry, Little Bit," he apologized. "I didn't want to ruin your honeymoon."

"You're not ruining my honeymoon," I said. "But how are we going to get plane tickets to Sydney so soon? The expense—"

"Jenna's bosses offered to let us use the company jet," Marv said. "They're worried about their employee as well, but it wouldn't look good if they were to start hunting for her. She works mostly from her Sydney apartment, but they haven't been able to get into contact with her. Because she's only a visitor in the country as well, the logistics of involving the authorities are a bit muddled."

I nodded my understanding, not liking the complexity of the situation. "We'll leave tomorrow then," I decided. "This will be good."

Knix glanced at me skeptically and in response, I squirmed in Texas' lap until he released me enough that I could climb over him and straight into Knix's lap—white ruffled skirts and all. I grabbed his face in one of my hands, tilting him gently to look up at me with my fingers on his jawline. "In fact, I think this is just the thing to excite me," I continued. I leaned down and pressed my lips to his for a chaste kiss before grinning and flopping down on his other side as I regarded everyone else in the limo. "Besides, Australia is exciting. I'm sure we'll find Clarissa's niece and make sure she's situated and safe and have some fun in the process." I smiled brightly as if to assure them that I was more than happy with this change of plans.

Marv and Grayson eyed me skeptically. "Um, not to be the bearer of bad news...again," Grayson started.

"But have you ever been to Australia?" Marv finished.

I shook my head. "Well, no, but—"

"Believe me," he interrupted, "it's hotter than Hades and everything is trying to kill you."

"I'm sure it's not that bad," I argued.

"It is that bad," Grayson agreed. "Why do you think Knix is so sorry?"

I looked back to Knix and then to Bellamy and Texas. "What about you two?" I asked.

They shrugged as one. "We've never been," Bellamy answered.

I spotted the venue as we approached and gathered my skirts closer to my legs as the limo slowed down. "It'll be fine," I said. "Every new place has interesting things that are just waiting to be discovered. I'm sure it won't be all that bad."

Marv shook his head in a negative and Grayson struggled to contain his amusement. "As much as I love to tell you when you're right, Babydoll," he said, "in this, you're wrong. In fact, if I didn't think you'd whoop my ass, I'd ask that you stay behind."

I narrowed my eyes on him in a glare. "You're right," I replied. "I would whoop your ass if you asked me to stay behind. If you're going then so am I."

Marv groaned and closed his eyes. "It'll be fine," I repeated, more sternly this time and as a last ditch effort to convince them that it wouldn't be as bad as they apparently thought, I spoke again. "It'll be great," I stubbornly insisted as we pulled to a stop outside the venue.

Bellamy, Texas, and Knix didn't reply, but Grayson and Marv both looked at me with sardonic amusement. "Whatever you say, Sunshine," Marv replied. "But when you eat your words later, don't get mad if we say 'I told you so.'"

Frowning, I let them exit the limo first before waiting for Knix to reach back in and hand me out onto the sidewalk. I was determined to make our trip to Sydney, Australia a success now. We'd find Clarissa's niece, keep her out of harm's way, and if all went according to plan—I might even be able to seduce my new husbands into spending more than a few hours in a hotel hot tub.

I grinned at the image that plan brought forth. *Yes, Australia was going to be great,* I decided.

CHAPTER 6

The first thing I noticed was the ungodly, awful wave of fiery torridity that slapped my cheeks the second we left the airport. The heat made my hair frizz and puff up and it was impossible to maintain. I yanked the strands back and struggled to get a hair tie off my wrist as we stopped on the platform where lines of people awaited approaching cars. I could feel a thick, clinging layer of heat settle on my skin, clogging up my pores. I grimaced and Grayson shot me a look of amusement.

"Shut up," I snapped, slapping his arm as I finished my task.

Putting his arms up defensively, he backed away still grinning. "I didn't say anything," he replied.

"You thought it," I growled, "loudly."

That made him laugh. "My goodness, you're positively violent this morning," he teased.

"I'm just tired," I said. "It was a long flight." It wasn't a lie. The flight from Charleston, South Carolina to Sydney,

Australia had been more than fifteen hours with a layover in Los Angeles. We hadn't so much as switched plans as we had switched pilots and had to wait for the jet to be refueled before we could reboard and head on our way. And sleeping on a plane rocketing through the night sky was just a smidge difficult. Even with a little melatonin, I had barely gotten more than three hours of sleep.

"Holy balls," Texas whined as he came through the sliding glass doors behind me. "This is worse than Charleston summers."

"It's called dry heat," Marv commented lightly as Knix strode to the end of the platform and hailed a cab.

"I feel like a wrinkling prune," Texas replied and I had to admit, I agreed. Not that I would admit it to Marv or especially Grayson.

"It's actually the winter months for Australians," Marv said lightly.

"Bullshit," Texas snapped, his jaw gaping in shock.

Marv nodded, a smile fighting at his lips. "Seriously."

Texas stared at him for a moment then turned to look at Grayson with a narrowed glare as if he was to blame for the weather before he finally gave in and turned away, muttering beneath his breath. "Fucking Australia," I heard him mumble as he bypassed me, and I stifled a giggle.

Knix came back momentarily and lifted the bag that I'd dropped at my feet along with his own as he turned towards an approaching taxi van. "I got it," I protested, reaching for the luggage—or at least my own. But in response, he turned and leaned down, silencing me with a kiss on my lips.

"Let me," he insisted, kissing me once more. I sighed against his mouth, my thoughts escaping like bats out of hell from my brain. He could have asked me what my name was in that moment and I would've been hard pressed to know the answer.

"You're horrible," I complained without heat when he finally proceeded to pull away.

Knix shrugged, his big shoulders lifting in a negligent fashion as he flashed me a grin and went to the van idling on the curb to stow away our bags. The guys followed after him, doing the same with their own luggage and we settled in for the ride to the hotel.

Even as Texas continued to complain about the heat in the backseat, I settled comfortably against Bellamy and stared out the window. The city of Sydney was large and as the car sped through the streets, through tunnels and under overhangs, my eyes ate it up.

"Clarissa and Alex still haven't heard from the girl, so when we get to the hotel," Knix spoke up, causing me to look to the front of the van where he sat alongside the driver, "I want Texas to contact Bricker and Stein, the branch office here, and see if he can get into their email system. I want to see what correspondence Clarissa's niece has had with the defendant."

"I won't need to contact them, I can get into it without their help," Texas replied lightly.

Knix sent him a reproachful glance over my head. "I want everything aboveboard," was all he said.

I peeked over my shoulder to see Texas' response, and he turned his head and saw me. Winking, he responded,

"Roger that, boss man. No illegal activities." He paused before adding, "For now…"

Knix ignored that last comment, turning his head to focus on Marv and Grayson. "I suspect you two already have an idea of where you want to start looking?"

Marv nodded. "The firm owns a few apartments in the city for when they have high profile clients or when they have executives visiting. She was put up in one of those. We'll take the taxi to the offices and get the key from her superiors before heading over and sussing it out."

Knix tipped his chin. "I'll come with you. I want to stay behind and go through her workspace to see if there is anything more we can figure out."

"What do you want me to do?" I asked.

Knix's blue eyes slid over me and a soft smile came to his lips. "Not sure yet, Little Bit. Just stay at the hotel with Bellamy and Tex and get settled. We'll talk more after we get a bearing on what we're dealing with."

I frowned. "I can help, you know," I said.

He shook his head. "I'm not doubting that," he replied. "But at the moment, everything is taken care of."

"I don't have anything to do, Sweetheart," Bellamy said, rubbing my thigh soothingly with one of his large palms. His rough, browned skin looked even darker against the pale flesh when I looked down at where his fingers trailed. "Keep me company," he said. "Just for today."

I sighed, giving in with an irritated harrumph. "You will let me know if there's something I can do, though," I replied. "Right?"

"We will, Sunshine," Marv answered, leaning up from where we sat in the back with Texas and Grayson.

My lips pulled into a straight line and I knew I didn't look convinced, but I also knew it was the best I would get from them. I forced myself to relax against Bellamy's hold as the taxi made its way through the new and foreign city.

CHAPTER 7

"Australia?" The word was hissed with no small amount of horror and trepidation. "When I said I wish you'd go on a more exotic location, I didn't mean going to a place where the sidewalk melts the soles of your shoes."

"It's not that bad," I insisted without much conviction. The heat had been pretty awful when I first landed. I paced between the sliding glass windows leading out onto our seventh floor balcony and one of the queen sized beds that divided the space between where I was wearing a hole in the hotel carpet and the rest of the space.

"Not that bad," Lizzie parroted.

I turned again and switched the phone to my other ear as I paused and looked across the room. Two queen sized beds, a pull-out couch and a large bathroom made up the majority of the room. The desk built into the wall across from the beds was overflowing with computer equipment. I didn't know how Texas had managed to get that much technology through customs, but no one had even bothered to check his bags. He had two laptops set up, their screens illuminated and flashing through a series of documents as he rapid-fire clicked across both of them.

I sighed when I realized Lizzie had yet to say anything more. "Lizzie?"

"I'm still here," she replied immediately sounding a bit winded.

"Are you okay?" I asked. "What—"

"No!" she snapped, interrupting my next question. "I am not okay. I'm still stuck on the fact that you're in Australia."

"What's wrong with Australia?" I asked a bit defensively. "It's perfectly nice."

"Perfectly nice?" she repeated.

"Are you going to copy everything I say for the entire duration of this conversation?" I inquired.

"No, of course not," she answered, "but you have to admit, I have a right to be shocked. The last time I talked to you, you were supposed to be heading to Key West. I don't know how bad you are at geography but Key West is most certainly not in Australia."

I winced before I even spoke—I knew what her reaction would be. "We decided to put off the honeymoon for another week or so," I said. "We have—"

"You *put off* your honeymoon?" she snapped. "Someone better be either dead or dying."

"They very well might be, you don't know that."

"Harlow," she sounded as though she were trying to hold in a mountain of emotions, "just tell me one thing."

Had she been in front of me, I would have squinted at her in suspicion. "What?" I asked hesitantly.

"Are you getting the dick?"

"Oh my God." I rolled my eyes heavenward.

"Please, please tell me you're at least having honeymoon sex even if you're not having a honeymoon," she persisted.

I shot a glance over my shoulder at where Bellamy exited the bathroom and then sprawled out on one of the mattresses. I bent my head and whirled to face the sliding glass doors before I hissed a response. "I swear to God," I started, "you are more obsessed with my sex life than—"

"I'm just trying to make sure you're taken care of," she defended, "You've got how many husbands? You better be getting some at least five times a week," she continued. "That's one man per day. I mean, I'd prefer for—"

"I'm hanging up," I cut her off. "I just wanted you to know where we were because I know you'll get pissed if you find out later and I didn't tell you."

"You're damned right I'd be pissed," she replied without shame. "I'm your best friend."

"Yes, you are. Now I gotta go."

"I hope it's so you can take a trip to *bone town!*"

I squeaked and jammed my finger against the end call, but it was too late, her last two words had been shrieked into the receiver and had definitely been more than audible. I turned, chancing a glance over my shoulder.

Both Texas and Bellamy had stopped and lifted their heads, turning in my direction. A flush stole over my cheeks, but I shoved down my irrational need to flee somewhere to live out the rest of my life as an embarrassed nun. Damn Lizzie.

Finally, the silence was broken by Bellamy's deep

chuckle. "Come on, Sweetheart," he said, rolling to his side and straight off the bed, bounding to his feet in one long elegant movement—like a cat falling from a great height, always landing on his feet. "Why don't we go down to the hotel pool."

Texas shot him a sharp look and his lower lip stuck out. Unable to help myself, I crossed the room towards him, sliding my arms around his shoulders as I leaned down and pressed a kiss to his lips. He lifted his head willingly, his mouth opening under mine. One hand came up and cupped the back of my head as he held me to him, his tongue seeking entrance that I gave up willingly. Sparks danced between us, and the longer we kissed, the more firmly his hold became.

When I managed to turn my cheek—needing oxygen—I found myself panting. "Go," I heard Texas say. "Lord knows I can't get shit done with you here, looking like that."

I frowned as he released me and I backed away, looking down at my shorts and tank top. "Looking like what?" I asked.

"Edible," he said, his eyes hot.

My blush took on a whole new meaning, but I nodded anyway and when Bellamy moved to take my hand, I let him. Texas turned back to his computers as Bellamy urged me into the bathroom to change and we headed down to the pool with towels in hand. Surprisingly, there wasn't a soul around as we climbed into the outdoor swimming pool, adjoined by a small circular jacuzzi hot tub.

"Do you think we'll be able to find Clarissa's niece?" I

asked after several minutes wading and floating in the crystal clear water. My voice echoed up in the empty space between the two wings of the hotel.

Something slithered by me and I tipped my head up, realizing that Bellamy had come nearer. His arms closed around me, lifting me against his naked torso. I looked up into his face. He considered the question with a peculiar expression, one that was unsure, but enigmatic at the same time.

"We will do the best we can, Sweetheart," he settled on saying.

I smiled, slipping my arms around his broad shoulders and linking my fingers behind his neck. Above us, twilight settled in an oversaturation of oranges, yellows, and reds. "It's only five o'clock," I said absently. "Why is the sun going down?"

"It's winter here," he reminded me. "It goes down earlier."

"It's weird to think of it as winter," I replied as he carried me through the water towards the steps leading out of the pool and into the hot tub. "It's still in the seventies."

He flashed me an amused grin. "One man's heat is another man's cold."

I pressed my lips together and lifted a brow. "You made that up," I accused.

His shoulders lifted in a shrug. "Does it make it any less true?" he asked.

Having no reply, I merely rolled my eyes and clenched my limbs as we finally lifted out of the water and my body settled against him—gravity pulling me down as the buoyancy of the water was left behind. I needn't have bothered though. Bellamy's hands on me were rock solid as he carried me the short two foot distance up the steps and into the jacuzzi. A breath hissed through my teeth as my skin met with the too-warm water and we sank down. I sighed and snuggled closer and together, we stared up and watched as the sun slowly sank down over the horizon.

I turned when the outside lights came on and started when I realized Bellamy's eyes were on me. Darkness had fallen over us and the only thing illuminating his face were the blurry yellowed lights in the corners of the outdoor area and the dim underwater bulbs beneath us. They reflected a strangeness in his features that made my breath catch as he lifted one hand out of the water. A finger stroked at the edge of my chest, just over my collarbone and under the string of my bikini.

"Bellamy?" I couldn't say why I thought it was necessary to whisper when there was no one nearby, but I felt even that was too loud.

"Do you know how precious you are to me?" he asked. Mute, I shook my head. A smile lifted the corners of his mouth as he leaned forward. A shiver stole up my spine as he pressed a chaste kiss to my temple before tilting his head to the side so that his lips rested right before my ear. "Should I show you?"

"What do you want to show me?" I asked, keeping my voice low.

His hand moved up to cup my chin as he pulled his head back. Dark brown eyes glittered with intent. "I want to show you the world," he said. "I want to lay dragons at your feet."

"There are no dragons," I replied.

White teeth flashed in a dark-skinned face. The olive tone of it was shadowed in the lack of light. He leaned forward and nipped my lower lip. I gasped, the sensation so abrupt that it made the entirety of my body arch upward in an automatic movement. "I think there are," he said, "and I think I'm one of them."

I mumbled something—though only God knew what it was. I meant for it to be encouragement though, and that intention obviously got through because he squeezed me closer. All I knew was that I had to kiss him. I turned fully, sliding one leg over his lap and anchoring myself up until I was pressed to him—his chest against my breasts. He bared his teeth as I settled on his lap, feeling how hard he was beneath me.

"Harlow…" My name on his lips was a plea, a demand. One I happily wanted to comply with. I let my eyes slide closed as my arms encircled his neck. My fingers sank into the long dark strands gathered together in a hair tie at the base of his neck.

When his lips met mine, they did so gently at first, rubbing with restraint. I didn't like that. I didn't want restraint. I wanted him unbound. I fisted the hair tie and tugged it down, tossing it away as I sank my other hand into his hair and held his skull roughly, slanting my mouth over his.

It must have sparked whatever vein of aggression some men had because, in the next instant, Bellamy stood up and slid me across the hot tub until I was seated and he was leaning over me, blocking out everything else. His lips captured mine with intent, his tongue sinking past any perceived resistance and *taking*.

Wide hands, rough from hard work, slid over my sides, beneath the triangles of fabric of my top. My nipples stiffened despite the heat of the water and beneath my bottoms, I knew the wetness gathering was due to more than just the hot tub. I moaned when strong fingers stroked against the tips of my breasts, and then when a thumb and forefinger latched onto one and pinched down lightly, I jerked. Water sloshed over the side of the small enclosure and my eyes shot open as a gasp left me.

"Harlow…" Bellamy's voice was gruff, a mere rasp in the darkness. I reached up and yanked him back down to my mouth as my chest arched forward, seeking more of that feeling. My legs scissored beneath the water. My tongue invaded his mouth, tasting him, loving him.

He continued to cup my breast in his palm, toying with my nipple in lazy simple movements that only served to heat my blood even more. I squirmed beneath him. It wasn't enough. I could have wept with relief when I felt his other hand start to trace a path up my thigh. My legs spread so swiftly that it left him breaking off the kiss and chuckling in amusement.

"Don't worry, Sweetheart," he said, pressing a kiss to my forehead. "I'll take care of you."

"*When?*" I demanded.

His chuckles turned into a low laugh. "We're in public," he chastised.

I chanced a glance around and then gave him a baleful glare. "There's no one else here."

"There are probably cameras," he said.

"So?" I replied tartly. "It's not like they'll be able to see anything."

His eyes widened and I knew I'd surprised him. In fact, I'd surprised myself. I wasn't usually so...adventurous. The fire of lust in my veins, however, was certainly entertaining the idea of doing it right here, out in the open, where anyone could walk by and see us. I knew Bellamy would shield me if anyone happened to come by, but the likelihood was low. We hadn't seen a soul out here since we had arrived.

"Don't tell me you're scared?" I challenged softly.

"Oh, Sweetheart." His gaze was dangerous as it slid over my face. "You could tempt a fucking eunuch."

"I don't want to tempt a fucking eunuch." I repeated his words with a grin. "I want to tempt you. Is it working?"

Another hard kiss jarred me. Our teeth clanked unevenly as the hand on my breast shot up and held my head steady for his onslaught. I opened willingly, moaning as he took control, pressing me back into the tiled wall. "Yes," he gasped, pulling away after a moment. "God, yes."

"Good," I whispered as I reached back and untied the knot holding my top up. I let it fall and relished the fire that grew in his eyes as he leaned forward and took one tender bud into his mouth.

With a sigh, I relaxed into his hold and let one of my hands drift up further into the strands of his hair, playing with them as he sucked my nipple between his teeth and bit down just enough for the pressure to send a shot of lust through my system. I groaned and wiggled against him.

"More," I begged. "I want more."

Bellamy reached beneath me and freed himself from the confines of his swim trunks. Strong fingers slid between my thighs, tugging the elastic fabric of my bikini bottoms to the side. His mouth released me as he lifted me up until I hovered a few inches above where his cock stood, tall and proud. And finally—*finally*—he lowered me down. I sank onto him, tightening as he pushed his way forward, powering into me.

"Bellamy…" I whispered his name as he buried his face in my neck and groaned. The vibrations of the needy sound sent me into overdrive. I clenched my muscles, eliciting another groan from him as I lifted up once more and slowly—oh so slowly—sank back down. I did this again, several times—each time more electric than the last.

I could feel my orgasm coming upon me like a freight train. I didn't want to stop it. Not when I felt how barely controlled Bellamy was—his muscles shaking beneath me as I slid my hands down letting them rest on his shoulders as I pushed up abruptly and dropped. His lips parted and my mouth sought him out.

He returned the kiss with enthusiasm, gripping me to him as he came undone. My breath caught as I felt it. He jerked inside me and I moaned as he reached down with one hand on my back and the other snaking down my stomach towards the bundle of nerves just above where he was connected with me. He rubbed that place, shooting off sparks in my mind—behind my eyelids as I shut them.

A wave of euphoria overtook me. I gasped, shuddered and let him catch me as I slowly fluttered back to Earth.

Panting and satisfied, he chuckled against my skin. "You are far too much, Sweetheart," he said.

I grinned, pressing a soft kiss to his neck as I turned my head. "I'm never too much for you," I whispered. Whether he agreed or not was lost, though, because the warmth of the water, combined with the feel of his naked skin against me was enough to lull me to sleep, my head pillowed between his chest and shoulder.

I should have been concerned about someone seeing me, but I wasn't. I was in Bellamy's arms and I knew that no matter what, he would take care of me.

CHAPTER 8

The scratching of pen on paper woke me. It was such an innocent sound—barely louder than someone's breath and yet the force and speed of it somehow broke its way through my dreams and pulled me up from unconsciousness. I blinked my eyes open and poked my head out from beneath the sheets I was under.

Early morning sunlight streamed in through the sliding glass doors. Texas sat at the hotel desk scratching his pen against a notebook as he looked up to one of his computer screens and then down again. I scanned the room, but it seemed like we were the only two here.

Peeking underneath the covers, I determined that Bellamy had given me one of his shirts to sleep in before he had mysteriously disappeared. I vaguely recalled him carrying me back to the room and him sitting me half up on the bed as he tugged a shirt over my head, though he'd left me in my now damp bikini bottoms.

"What are you doing?" I mumbled as I yawned and stretched.

Texas' scribbling paused and his head slowly came up. "Hey, you're awake." He smiled as I slipped out of the covers and made my way across the room.

I paused at his side and looked down, not quite sure what I was seeing. There were notes, numbers, dates, times, names of places I didn't recognize, and arrows drawn through the margins. "What is this?" I asked. "Where are the others?"

"Knix found something at Jenna's office. He called Bellamy to go with him. Marv and—"

"Did they not come back?" I was shocked. *Had I not heard them?*

"You were out," Texas said. "Jetlag's a bitch. The guys came back and caught a couple of hours each before they headed out again.

"Okay, so...you said Bellamy's with Knix?" I asked, glancing back to the desk.

He nodded, reaching over and closing the notebook as he stood up. "Yup, and now that you're up, we should probably get ready to meet them."

I blinked as he took the notebook and moved to the bed furthest away from the balcony, but followed anyway and reached between the mattresses for my bag as I rifled through it and pulled out clothes. I kept him in my sights as I changed, watching as he clicked away on his phone, keeping the notebook at his side.

"I called for a ride," he said when I finished. "They're here."

"Where are we going?" I asked as we headed for the hallway.

"Knix and Bellamy are at Bricker and Stein. We'll meet

them there. They might have found something that can lead to Jenna's whereabouts."

I nodded and followed him out of our room, into the elevator, through the lobby, and out onto the streets, where a tinted blue sedan waited on the curb, it's hazards flashing. We got into the backseat, Texas murmuring instructions as I scooted across to the other side. It wasn't until we were well on our way that I prompted him about the notebook.

"What's that?" I asked.

Texas glanced down as I gestured to where it sat in his lap. "I called Bricker and Stein last night while you and Bellamy were down by the pool,"—try as I might, I couldn't stop the blush from coming to my cheeks, but if he noticed, he didn't comment—"and they gave me access to security camera footage as well as Jenna's timecard."

I cleared my throat. "And they just gave it to you?"

He grinned boyishly. "I might have led them to believe that their home office had hired me as a PI to search for their missing employee. It's not completely a lie," he went on when I pursed my lips at him. "We are looking for her."

"PI?" I said. "How are we going to prove that if we need to?"

"Bellamy actually is a licensed private investigator."

"He is?" I blinked. "I didn't know that."

"Well…" Texas' smile grew.

I narrowed my eyes on him. "What?" When he didn't immediately answer me, I reached over and touched the notebook. "Don't make me take this, you still haven't answered my questions."

"He's only licensed in the United States," Texas admitted.

I huffed. "And the notebook?"

"Notes," he said. "On the case. I dated all of the times I saw Jenna's face on the security footage and correlated it with her timecards. I got a picture of her employee ID from the office as well. From there, I hacked into the cities' CCTV and followed her—"

"CCTV?" I shook my head. "What's that?"

"CCTV is closed circuit television. It's video recording in public areas, usually reserved for following crime and tracking down perpetrators," Texas explained.

"Okay." I nodded. "And you followed her using that?"

He nodded, but just as he opened his mouth to go on, the car pulled up to a curb outside of a tall office building and the driver announced our arrival. "Thanks," Texas said, reaching forward and handing the man a few bills before we got out. "Let's get inside and find the others before we continue this conversation," he suggested.

I glanced up as the hot Australian sun burned across my cheeks and forehead and squinted at the reflective surface of the building as we strode for the spinning front doors. Texas didn't even hesitate as we walked into the chrome and glass interior, moving through the lobby with confidence as he approached the front desk. I hung back for a moment as he spoke to the woman sitting there with her strawberry blonde hair pulled back into a severe bun.

My eyes scanned the room, noting the men in business suits and searching for the cameras Texas had mentioned. I spotted a couple above the front entrance, as well as over by the elevators, among other places. If Jenna had come to the office regularly, there was no doubt in my mind that her timecard would have had to correlate with her arrival and departure times. Unless there were other unseen entrances, there was no way to get in and out of the building without being seen by at least one security camera.

Texas' hand touched my elbow, startling me as he urged me towards the elevators. "They're upstairs in the meeting room."

"Marv and Grayson?" I asked.

He nodded. "Everyone's here. They're there with Jenna's temporary supervisor."

We took the elevator up to the fifth floor and when the doors slid open, I saw the top of Marv's golden-blond head. The meeting room was across from the elevators, the clean hallway windows allowing me to see him as he paced back and forth parallel to a long table. Texas and I moved towards the door of the room where the guys and another man I didn't recognize were quietly talking.

Knix's head popped up as we entered, but before he or I could say anything, Texas went down the row of windows looking out into the hall and lowered all the blinds.

"What's going on?" Knix demanded as I went to his side. His hand moved to the small of my back, sending a shiver up my spine.

"I'm not sure," I answered. "Texas said he might have found something. Did you find anything?"

He looked down at me, his expression softening before he sighed and shook his head. "I had to ask Bellamy to track down a few notes from people she had been talking to, but other than that, all we managed to discover is that she didn't keep her case notes in the office."

"Of course not," the stranger said—I assumed this was the supervisor Texas had mentioned. He was a tall, thin man with a bushy mustache tipped in gray. It fluttered as he blew out a breath. "Jenna was working from the apartment for most of her stay here."

"Why?" I asked. "Wouldn't you want confidential information kept in the office?"

"Everything Jenna was working on was done via computer. Any confidential information she had was password protected on a company laptop."

"Is this the laptop?" Texas asked as he stopped by the table and gestured for the silver cased laptop sitting there.

The man nodded.

"We found it in the apartment and brought it here when Knix called us and told us to meet here," Grayson said.

Texas moved to open it as he set the notebook down. "Like I said, it's password protected," the supervisor warned. "The only people to know the password were Jenna and my boss."

"Why is that, Mr. Stover?" Knix asked. "You are her supervisor, shouldn't you have her password."

Marv paused in his pacing as the man answered. "Normally, I would have, but Jenna was a temporary employee from another branch. My boss is her main supervisor, I was simply her liaison and supervisor when he was out."

"Which he is today," Bellamy pointed out.

Mr. Stover nodded, and a moment later, Texas looked up from the laptop. "I'm in."

The man's eyes widened and he hurried around Texas' other side, gaping at the screen he saw. "That's not—you shouldn't be able to—how did you—"

"Most people don't use random digits or words for their passwords," Texas explained. "So, if you know a little bit about the person, it helps to be able to hack their accounts. I've spent the last several hours learning as much as I could about Jenna Wiedleman's habits. Her password is pretty simple."

"But…" The man continued to stare at the screen as Texas clicked through documents and opened up tabs. "You're in company documents. Those should have been sealed."

"Companies are harder," Texas admitted without pulling his gaze away from what he was doing. "But they're all pretty much the same. They need a seemingly random way to track company documents. The password was a combination of Jenna's employee ID as well as her American social security number—I figured it out since most of these documents are from the primary branch. She only came here because the man she's attempting to prosecute is native to Australia. From what I read on the documents detailing the lawsuit, he claimed to have been in Australia during the time the embezzled funds were transferred to a Swiss bank account with a surprisingly unoriginal name attached: John Smith." Texas sighed as if disappointed and I had to bite my lip to keep from laughing. "Some people have no imagination."

"Texas," Marv snapped. "What did you find?"

"Well, nothing much from the documents on here or that I managed to gain access to via the company employee system your boss"—Texas paused to gesture to Mr. Stover—"gave me permission to hack."

"He gave you permission to hack into sensitive company documents?" Mr. Stover looked ready to faint. "No, he couldn't have. He wouldn't—"

"To be fair," Texas interrupted, "I did challenge him and he didn't think I could really do it."

"I recall telling you to keep everything above board," Knix said on a sigh.

"It is above board," Texas argued. "The primary owner and partner of Bricker and Stein gave me the go-ahead."

"Did he really do that or did you goad him into it?" Bellamy asked.

"Does it matter?"

When Knix pinched the bridge of his nose and took a long, steady breath, I decided that enough was enough. Touching Knix's arm and smoothing a hand down his bicep reassuringly, I looked towards Texas. "Tell us what you found," I said.

Texas nodded and went back to scrolling through documents and moving them around for a second before he flipped open the notebook and began to type rapidly, scanning the scribbles on the page briefly as he began to speak again. "When I couldn't get much other than a background through the company documents on the case Jenna was working, I looked through security footage and correlated her timecard to where she appeared on the cameras. Then I followed her on the last day she was seen using CCTV technology."

"Did you find her?" Mr. Stover asked, appearing pale.

Bellamy moved towards the older gentleman and pulled out a chair, urging the man to sit.

"I didn't." Texas sounded frustrated by that fact. I could just imagine that he was too. All of this sounded rather advanced, but if it hadn't gotten us to our goal—which was finding Jenna—then we were still in the dark. "But I did find a few places she visited before she was supposed to have returned home."

Marv moved around the back of Texas' chair and watched as Texas typed a few things in and scrolled across whatever he was looking at before clicking sharply and sitting back. "That's her," Marv said.

Grayson strode across the room and looked as well. "Is this time stamped correctly?" he asked.

Texas nodded and then turned the screen for the rest of us to see. It was a grainy still of a short, dark skinned woman in a business suit, holding a briefcase as she got into a dark towncar.

Knix released me and put his hands on the table, leaning over as he stared at the image. "Can you pull the license plate numbers?" he asked.

"Of course." Texas turned the laptop back, clicked a few buttons, flipped to a new page in his notebook and scribbled something down before ripping it out and handing it over.

Knix took the paper and frowned down at the numbers. "Okay, Texas, you and I will take this and head back to the hotel. We'll find the owner of this vehicle and track him down. Bellamy, can you stay here with Mr. Stover and as soon as they're awake, call Clarissa and give her and Alex an update."

Bellamy nodded and Mr. Stover looked wilted and tired. I felt bad for the poor man as he shakily tried to stand. "Jenna is a wonderful employee, but have you ever considered that she decided to go into hiding because of the threats?" he asked. "Or perhaps she was bought off and used the money to disappear."

I frowned. "Bought off?" I asked.

Mr. Stover looked at me, his lips tilting down. I could tell he didn't appear to like my presence and he proved it in the next moment. "I'm sorry, but who are you?" he demanded.

"This is my wife," Knix said.

My whole body tightened at the announcement. Not that it wasn't true, but was still so new to hear it. The word sent a ripple of pleasure through me—completely inappropriate in timing, but undeniable.

"And is your wife in any way qualified to deal with issues of this magnitude?" Mr. Stover inquired sharply.

My eyebrows shot up even before Knix answered. "She is a part of my team, Mr. Stover," Knix replied. "And as far as I see it, we've done more to look for your employee than you have. If I deem she's qualified, then she is."

While I appreciated that Knix was standing up for me, the truth was I still hadn't done anything in the way of looking for Jenna. I kept my lips sealed, though, and waited.

Eyeing me with a mixture of doubt and distaste, Mr. Stover's lips curled, but he let the matter rest as he turned back to Texas. "I'd like for any and all information you have on this manner to be sent to me directly, Mister…?"

"Johnson," Texas answered.

"Mr. Johnson, if you would be so kind as to send me everything you have."

Texas glanced to Knix, and there was a brief pause of tension as I watched anger flare to life in Mr. Stover's expression. Before anything could happen, Knix sighed and nodded. "Give it to him," he said.

Texas nodded and clicked through a few things on the laptop. "Alright, it's sent."

"Thank you," Mr. Stover said stiffly. "I think I can trust that you'll see yourselves out. I'll be returning to my office. Please keep me abreast of any further discoveries."

"Will do, Mr. Stover," Knix said.

The older man nodded, cast me a sharp glance, and then departed.

"Well, he's a ball of sunshine," Texas said dryly.

"Ignore him," Knix said. "We've got more important things to do."

"Do you still want me to stay here?" Bellamy asked.

Knix nodded. "Keep an eye on Stover and go back through Jenna's office space. Interview employees. Find out if she went out with any of her coworkers here. If they knew anything about her casework."

"Will do." Bellamy passed by me, pausing to press a kiss to my forehead before he disappeared out the door.

"I'll still be going back to the hotel with Texas and once we have the owner of the car's name, we'll head out and track him down." Knix straightened away from the table. "Where else did she go on the day before she went missing?"

Texas scribbled a few things down in his notebook and

tore off two slips of paper. "Just two places—a coffee shop and a bank."

"Alright," Knix nodded to Grayson. "You take the bank. Ask for their security footage and see when she was there and who she spoke with. Interview employees."

"Will do." Grayson took the slip of paper Texas held up and winked at me as he, too, walked out.

"What about me?" I asked.

"We'll take the coffee shop," Marv said, snatching the last slip of paper from Texas' hand before coming to stand at my side. "And we'll reconvene later tonight."

"Alright, keep me updated," Knix agreed.

Marv took my hand, but before I let myself be dragged out, I pulled to a stop in front of Knix and went on my tiptoes. Knix stared down at me before a soft smile graced his lips. He bent down to meet me halfway and brushed a soft kiss across my lips.

"Be careful," he whispered.

"Always," I promised just before I retook Marv's hand and we strode out of the meeting room. Hopefully, by this time tomorrow, we'd know exactly where Jenna had gone and would be well on our way to getting her back.

CHAPTER 9

Marv and I strode into *Bean Water*—one of the last places Clarissa's niece had been seen—and promptly headed for the countertop where a bright-smiled barista in a black and purple uniform welcomed us.

"Hi and welcome to *Bean Water,* what can I get for you today?"

"Actually, we're looking for someone and we're wanting to know if you've seen her," Marv said. "She's about this high"—he held up his hand just above my head—"and she's been missing for a few days. She's a dark skinned woman and she would've been wearing a business suit when she last came to this establishment." I grimaced. The barista began to frown, taking a step back from the counter as Marv's tone became more severe. "Have you seen her?"

"I-I don't—"

"Here, let me," I said with a sigh, moving to stand in front of Marv. "Hi"—I paused and glanced down at the woman's name tag—"Claire. My boyfriend and I were in here a few days ago and we ran into a woman on our way out and duh—stupid me, I made her spill all of the stuff she was carrying." I slapped my forehead playfully. "I accidentally crashed into her and her stuff got mixed with mine. It looks like I have everything I need, but I accidentally picked up some documents she had with her and they seem pretty important, but we're from America and we're about to leave to head home and we were hoping to find her and return her stuff. Can you just tell us if you've seen anyone matching her description?"

"There are a lot of people that come through here," the woman said, though she seemed more comfortable as I took the lead.

"Oh dang it, you probably do." I sighed and then winced as I looked back up at her. "Would we be able to speak to a manager about security footage? I'm sure you caught our accident on camera. Maybe if we point her out you can tell us if she's a regular here or we can at least print out a picture to give to the police if we have to give them her stuff before we leave the country."

"Oh, yeah." Relief was clear in her tone. "Let me go grab my manager!"

She dashed away as I stepped back and looked back at Marv. He lifted a brow at me. "You scare people when you're so serious," I said.

"Apparently," he agreed, "but there's just one thing wrong with your story."

"What? The fact that it's made up?" I asked.

He shook his head. "No." His hand gripped my hip and brought me closer as he leaned over and lowered his head until his mouth hovered over mine. I inhaled sharply. "I'm not your boyfriend, Sunshine." My heart pounded. "I'm your *husband*."

"I—"

"Hi, I'm the manager here at *Bean Water*, how can I help you, folks?"

I spun away from Marv and plastered a smile on my face as a short voluptuous woman with bright orange hair approached us. "Hi," I squeaked, shuffling away from Marv. I heard the quiet vibration of his chuckle at my back and quickly jerked my elbow back, nailing him in the side as I relayed the same story I had told the barista.

The manager—her name tag read Maria—frowned. "Normally, we don't let anyone look at security camera footage," she started. "But from what I understand, these are extenuating circumstances. When did you say you were leaving the country?"

I bit my lip. I knew it didn't matter if she didn't let us look at them. Texas could hack in when we got back to the hotel, but I also knew Knix wanted to keep everything as legal as possible.

"Two days," Marv answered. "We've been here for a while and we have to get back for work."

Maria nodded and when she agreed to let us in the back to look at security footage, I released a sigh of relief. "Thank you so much," I said.

"You go on ahead," Marv said as Maria moved towards the back office, gesturing for us to follow. "I'm going to check something out real quick."

I frowned his way, but before I could say anything, he

disappeared into the line of people who had begun to congregate at the counter as they ordered their drinks.

"This way please." I nodded and trailed after the *Bean Water* manager as she led me towards the back through a small kitchen and into an office with tiled floors and a poster of a large Italian man with a handlebar mustache, holding a minuscule porcelain cup of espresso. "All of the security footage gets sent to the main computer," Maria explained as she quickly scurried over to a small step ladder and adjusted it so that it was in front of the desk before she took the overstuffed looking computer chair.

I smiled and quietly nudged the stepladder back in place and came to stand alongside her as she clicked through some old files and found the security footage we needed. I gave her the date and time and she pulled up the video. I watched in silence as the frames moved by. I sighed when I noticed that the timeframe was stamped wrong—it was the right day, but the wrong time. The manager had pulled up the a.m. time period rather than the p.m. one I needed.

"Do you mind if I try?" I asked.

She looked up and scooted her chair back, nodding for the computer. Relieved, I leaned over and moved the mouse down to the times and moved up until it was past mid-afternoon. Slowing down the frames, I let it run for a few minutes before I saw the same woman Texas had pulled up a picture of on the security footage from Bricker and Stein.

I watched the woman on the screen for several long minutes, screenshotting a few of the frames. As accommodating as Maria was, I hesitated to ask for the full footage, so I asked if I could print off some of the screenshot frames. By the time those were done printing, Marv still hadn't come back so I thanked the woman and headed to the front, folding the images I had taken and tucking them into my back pocket.

Anxiety began to work its way through me when I saw that Marv was nowhere to be seen in the shop. Pulling my phone out, I stepped into the bright sunlight and took a path to the side, scrolling through to his number as I paused in the mouth of an alleyway, but a figure leaning over and talking to a gruff-looking homeless man had me putting my phone away and approaching cautiously.

Marv noticed my arrival and nodded, quietly thanking the man on the ground, half shaded by a cardboard overhang that was obviously self-built. Marv passed the man a few bills and turned, heading my way before I was even halfway over.

"Did you find out anything?" I asked, tucking my cell phone away.

Marv nodded. "Not here," he said, taking my elbow and urging me out onto the main stretch of road. He waited until he had flagged down a taxi and nudged me inside before he spoke. "That man's name is Gadson and Jenna spoke with him every time she visited *Bean Water*," Marv relayed.

"Did he see anything?" I asked. The car we were in turned onto the highway and jostled a bit, causing me to slide a bit closer as Marv shook his head.

He reached out and hooked his hand around the curve of my waist and brought me even closer as he spoke. "No, he didn't see her disappear—we've already determined that a car picked her up and to our knowledge, that car never made it to her destination."

"So why—"

Marv pressed two fingers against my lips, halting my questions as he smiled. "Let me finish, Sunshine," he said. "I promise I'll tell you everything I know, okay?" I blushed, but nodded nonetheless, settling against him with an expectant expression. He chuckled before sobering. "I spoke with Gadson because a lot of people don't see the homeless as actual people. They don't realize that these men and women can see and hear just as well as anyone else. They're actually pretty amazing in their ability to seem anonymous and remain hidden and practically invisible in plain sight. I asked if Gadson had seen Jenna on the day she disappeared, he admitted that he had, but he didn't see any car that had taken her."

"So we're back to where we started." I sighed.

Marv shook his head. "Not completely. I asked if Gadson had seen anyone on any of the previous occasions that she'd stopped to talk to him. If she stopped to see him every time she went to *Bean Water*, there's a likely chance he might have seen someone involved in her disappearance."

"Why would you think that?" I asked, my brows puckering with confusion.

Marv lifted his head and stared out the back window of the car as he continued. "Usually when someone disappears, they're taken by someone they know. Right now, we're assuming that the man responsible for taking Jenna is involved in the lawsuit case for embezzlement she was working on before she vanished."

I bit my lip, sliding my palm up his forearm as I moved in and pressed against his side. "Then shouldn't we be looking at him?" I asked. "It makes sense to determine his whereabouts and figure out if there's some place he could be holding her."

Marv nodded without looking down. "We've been keeping an eye on him—Texas has anyway. His name is Karl Tennison, and so far, he's maintained the same schedule he ever has without any deviation." Marv paused, a scowl gracing his lips. "He's disgustingly routine," he admitted. "If he's responsible or even involved in her disappearance, then he's hired outside help to do it."

The car pulled off the highway and turned onto the same street as our hotel. I waited until Marv had leaned up and paid the man and we both got out before asking the question rattling around in my skull. "How did you know to ask Gadson?" I blurted as Marv took my hand and led me through the front glass doors.

Marv shot me a grin. "I know Clarissa," he said, stopping in front of the elevators and pushing the button, "and I figured if her niece was anything like her then Jenna would make time to talk to people everyone else ignored. She's a kind soul."

I frowned. "She seems to be in a bad profession if that's the kind of person she is," I commented.

"Not necessarily," Marv argued as we stepped inside and the elevator doors slid closed. "Many people get into law because they want to help others. They want to right wrongs and exact justice in their own way."

I released his hand and scrubbed my palms down my

face, groaning in frustration. "We still don't know where she is and we haven't gotten much closer to finding her."

Marv moved closer, turning and pressing his back next to mine against the wall. "We'll find her, Sunshine," he said quietly after a moment. "You have to believe that."

"The first seventy-two hours are the most important in a missing person's case," I said. "We've bypassed that. How likely are our chances?"

I remembered how good Clarissa had been to me in the beginning of my relationship with the guys. I recalled how nice she'd been, how helpful. I didn't want to let her down and the further into this we got, the more anxious I grew. I worried we weren't going to be able to find Jenna Wiedleman, and I didn't want to be the person to tell Clarissa we had failed her.

"Hey," Marv reached out, turning me towards him, "we're going to find her. Don't worry. We've already come so far and we've only been here for a few days."

"I know," I said, but I was still unconvinced and he must have seen that on my face because he abruptly pulled me into his chest, squeezing me close.

His breath brushed over the top of my head. "I'm sorry," he whispered against my hair. "I know this isn't what—" The elevator dinged, interrupting whatever he had been about to say. I pushed back slightly, trying for a smile and a small shake of my head before I exited the elevator and headed for the hotel room. "Harlow," Marv called.

I pulled out the keycard, inserted it, and quickly jerked it back out. "It's fine," I called over my shoulder, turning the handle and pushing into the room. "I'm just worried about her is all."

Marv paused just behind me as the door swung inward to an empty space. I sighed, spotting the note from Knix and Texas on the desk. I moved towards it, unfolding the paper with the word 'read this' scribbled across its face.

On our way to speak with the owner of the car. Will call with any new information. Be back soon.

— Knix

I set the paper down and strode across the room, sinking onto the furthest bed. At least some of us had gotten good leads. Marv picked up the note and read over the words before he flashed me a look. Hopefully, they would have better luck than we'd had.

But what else could I do? I wondered. I laid back, closing my eyes as my mind raced. I started when the papers I had shoved into my back pocket poked me. Opening my eyes and sitting back up, I pulled them out and smoothed their edges.

"Harlow?" Marv's voice drew my gaze. I looked up at him before glancing back down at the papers.

"Here," I said, holding out the images. "I got these off of the security footage at *Bean Water*." Marv took them and set them to the side without looking at them. I frowned. "You should look through them," I said. "I wanted to get the video footage, but I didn't want to push our luck. Texas can probably get it later."

"I'll review them later," Marv said, moving until he stood in front of me, staring down as I tilted my face back to meet his eyes. "You didn't let me finish in the elevator."

"I knew what you were going to say," I replied.

"We feel bad that you had to come do this with us instead of going on your honeymoon."

The corner of my mouth twitched. "It would've been your honeymoon too," I pointed out. "And I didn't *have* to come; I came because I wanted to help."

"You're worrying we won't find her." His hands came down on my shoulders, moving until his thumbs dipped into the wide collar of my t-shirt, smoothing across my skin. A low simmering heat started up low in my abdomen as I gazed up into his murky gray eyes. "But we will," he continued, "and everything will work out."

I didn't say anything. I didn't want to contradict him because I hoped he was right even if I didn't have the same amount of hope. Instead, I watched as the low simmer I was feeling somehow began to burn within him. I continued to stare back as he leaned down, drawing closer and closer until he blocked out the rest of the room with his body. Until it felt like it was just me and him—we were the only ones and the world narrowed down to just the two of us.

CHAPTER 10

He lifted his palms and cupped my cheeks gently— holding them between his palms as his eyes roved over my face. He held me as if I were something precious—as if I were as valuable as a rare gemstone. Perhaps, more so. I let my eyes slide shut when he bent forward.

"Harlow…" I expected the feel of his lips against mine, but when they never came, my eyes shot open and my lips turned down. Eyes the color of thunderclouds bored into me. I jerked, nearly tearing myself from his grip. "Do you trust me?" he asked. I licked suddenly dry lips and nodded. "Can you say it?"

"I trust you, Marv," I said.

"Good," he replied. "Then trust that no matter what happens, we'll find Jenna and we'll work out everything else."

"You can't promise something like that," I warned him. "There are always going to be things beyond your control."

"Are you kidding me?" One corner of his mouth lifted into a rueful grin. "I'm all powerful, Sunshine."

I groaned. "You sound like Texas or Grayson."

His eyes flashed—lightning behind the clouds. "I guess they're finally rubbing off on me," he said just before he swooped down and took my lips. I sucked in a breath, my lips parting automatically and he took full advantage.

His hands cupped the sides of my head, holding me still as he invaded my mouth. A moan worked its way up my throat as that low simmering heat came to a fast boil. I reached for him, snaking my hands over his shoulders as I gripped fistfuls of his shirt and tugged upward.

Marv broke the kiss and quickly ripped off the shirt before nudging me up on the bed, his hands going to the waistband of my shorts. He took them and my underwear down, pulling them until they were free from my legs and sandals. Chuckling to himself in a deep reverberation, he gently slid fingers beneath the straps of my shoes and removed them as well.

Tossing them away, he put one knee on the bed. I stopped him with a hand on his bare chest. "If you get on this bed," I warned. "I'm going to want you. Take off your pants."

Marv's eyes widened at my daring, but when my fingers went to the hem of my own t-shirt and I whipped it over my head throwing it to the side, he quickly moved to follow my commands. He shucked his jeans down his legs and crawled onto the bed as I fiddled with my bra—struggling in my haste to get it off.

He moved over me, pressing a soft kiss to the bare skin of my shoulder as he reached behind me and deftly flicked the snaps of my bra open and pulled the straps down my arms. "As sexy as I think you are in your underwear," he whispered against my skin, sending goosebumps trailing up my arms and down my chest, "I like it even better when you have nothing separating us."

I spread my legs, letting him settle between them as I reached up and cupped his jaw, nudging him gently with my nose until I could kiss him the way I wanted to—slowly, reverently, torturously. I was practically vibrating with my need for him. I wanted him as I wanted nothing else. His love was my drug—an addiction from which I never wanted to be cured.

"Harlow...Sunshine..." His rough voice shivered along my spine. His fingers sank into my hair, holding on as he angled my head back and licked at my bottom lip.

I sighed into his mouth and pushed up with one hand flat on the bed, the tips of my breasts brushing against his chest. One of the hands against my face left and trailed down to feather across one of my nipples as he cupped me and leveraged himself more firmly against me. The heat of him burned up the inside of my thighs as he nudged my entrance and then slipped inside.

I whimpered at the feel of him, tearing my lips away as I panted. "Hold onto me," he urged, reaching for my wrist and tugging it up to his neck. I moved as he commanded, wrapping my arms more tightly around him until I clung to him. Only then did he roll and swing me so that I was on top and he sank even further than I thought was possible as I sat up.

Pleasure rolled through me, heating my skin and bringing a light pink flush to my cheeks. Marv's eyes glimmered with something I couldn't discern as he fingered the ends of my hair and gazed up at me through hooded lids. "Move, Sunshine," he said, tilting his hips so that he slid out just a bit before he canted them up and shoved inward once more.

My muscles tightened. "Marv." I gasped his name, reaching for something to hold onto. He put his palms out. Our fingers connected lacing together and I used the grasp I had on him to lift up and drop down.

The first thrust made my mouth pop open and shape into the form of an 'o.' "Do that again," I commanded, drawing a low chuckle from his chest.

But he acquiesced to my demand and pulled out slightly only to surge back in with a rough force. We repeated the motion, letting the swell of pleasure rise and rise until it crashed over us. I heard the depth of his groan as he went rock hard and froze. All the while, my muscles clenched and unclenched in jerky, spasming movements. My skin came alive with sensation until it felt as though I were overwhelmed by everything from his touch to the sunlight coming in from the windows.

I sighed once it had passed and sank down more fully, resting my head against his chest as we both breathed hard. Our breaths came heavy and panting, puffing out in long drags. "How can it feel like that every time?" I asked, wonder in my tone.

I felt Marv's smile against my forehead. "Because it's you," he replied. "It's never been like that with anyone else and I don't think it'll ever be. I'll hazard a guess that it's the same for the others. The common denominator is you, Sunshine."

"I'm not special," I protested.

Marv tugged a lock of my hair in retaliation. "Lies," he hissed between his teeth as I shifted and he slipped out. "I...shit," Marv cursed as he realized something I already knew. "I didn't use a condom," he said. "I'm sorry, Sunshine. I didn't think, I—"

"It's okay," I said, pulling back. "Bellamy and I—we...the other night, I mean—we didn't either."

Marv's expression darkened. "I should have thought—we both should have, him and I. It won't happen again."

I frowned and thought about it. "Why?" I asked, tilting my head. "I mean, I'm on birth control now, but even if I wasn't...I mean, we're married. Would it really be the worst thing in the world?" Marv looked dumbstruck and my stomach sank. "I mean, we should be fine, so there's nothing to worry about," I rushed to say. "Birth control—"

"It wouldn't be bad at all, Harlow," he interrupted me with a shake of his head. "Seeing you—having a son or a daughter with you—it's...I can't even describe the feeling...Harlow, if you get pregnant, it would be the most magical thing in the world. I love you."

Slowly, my anxiety faded. I took a deep breath. "I'm not sure if I'm ready, but if it's with you or one of the guys...I wouldn't...it would be...I think I'd be okay with it," I finally said. Marv blinked as I bent and pressed a light kiss to his lips. I pulled back with a grin. "I think we're okay for now, though."

"I'll be more careful next time," he promised. "But whenever you're ready…" He let the sentence trail off, but the meaning was clear. I nodded and slid off of him.

"We should get showered and dressed," I suggested.

"Knix and Texas will probably be back soon with more information."

He nodded his agreement, and I went to the bathroom. As the door clicked shut behind me, I pressed back against it and took a deep breath, releasing it on a slow exhale. A kid. With Marv or one of the others...the very thought sent butterflies dancing around in my stomach. I couldn't deny that I wanted it—but when we were all ready.

I'd be more careful in the future, I decided, *until the guys and I had a chance to talk about it more.*

A little over an hour after Marv and I had showered, dressed, and eaten—the hotel room door beeped and clicked open. Knix stepped inside, ducking beneath the doorway a smidge as he usually did to keep from hitting the top of the doorframe. I sat up and Marv came back in from the balcony as Bellamy, Grayson, and Texas stepped in behind Knix and closed the door.

"What happened?" I asked. "Did you find out anything?" My eyes moved from Grayson to Bellamy and back to Texas and Knix, but all four of them shook their heads. My shoulders drooped.

"The owner of the car that picked up Jenna but never dropped her off is Thomas Ollison," Knix said as everyone came in and spread out around the room. Bellamy and Texas dropped onto the opposite bed, Knix stood, and Grayson took the chair at the desk across from where I sat. "Texas and I tracked down his whereabouts—he lives in an apartment complex outside of the city limits—but he wasn't home."

"There was nothing more I could find in her office, and Mr. Stover finished out his work and went home without incident," Bellamy said.

Knix looked to Grayson next. "Anything on your end?"

Grayson shook his head. "No, they wouldn't even let me review the security tapes," he said. "I've spent the last several hours arguing with branch managers."

Knix sighed. "I was afraid of that."

"Do you want me to hack them?" Texas asked. "I know you didn't want to resort to that, but—"

Knix shook his head. "Anything we find illegally can't be used in court," he said.

"Are we going to court?" Texas asked with a frown as he tilted his head and cracked his neck. "I was under the impression that our main goal was to find Jenna Wiedleman."

"But she's involved in a very high profile embezzling case," Knix reminded him. "It's likely that this is all connected to that."

"But there's nothing we have on the man who's being prosecuted," Bellamy pointed out.

Knix pinched the bridge of his nose and blew out a breath, releasing it before nodding. "Yes, I know."

"We looked at the security footage from the coffee shop," I said, drawing everyone's attention. "I didn't think they'd let us take the video, but I was able to screenshot some of the images where Jenna appeared." I turned and searched for where Marv had put them earlier, finding them across from me on the desk behind Marv. I stood up

FOREVER & ALWAYS

and reached for them, unfolding them and handing them over. "Maybe they'd be helpful," I said hopefully.

"Thank you, Little Bit." Knix bent down and kissed the top of my head as he took the images from me. "For now, I think I need to send someone over to stakeout Ollison's apartment." He straightened, still clutching the papers in his fist. "We don't know when the man will return, but we want to be ready for him if or when he does."

"How long do you want to keep watch?" Marv asked.

"At least overnight, though I'd prefer a couple of days with rotating shifts," Knix answered.

"I can take a shift," I offered.

"I'll take—" Knix stopped when Marv stepped forward and put a hand on his arm.

"You need to get some rest," Marv said. "You've hardly slept since we got here. Stay behind for the next six to eight hours and get some sleep. Texas and Harlow will take the first shift. Bellamy and I will take the next and when you're rested up, you and Grayson can follow up with the third—unless Ollison shows himself before then."

I glanced between the two of them. Knix's face tightened in displeasure. I could tell he didn't want to agree, but there were bags under his eyes and a strain to his features that told me Marv was right.

"I think he's right," I agreed. "Texas and I will take first shift. We'll be fine."

Tense silence followed my words and it felt like an eternity until his shoulders drooped and the pressure seemed to lift from his body. "I don't expect Ollison will show up in the next few hours, but we need to keep a lookout for him just in case. You're right," he said, looking from me to Marv. "I'll stay behind and then come out later."

Marv clapped him on the back. "Good idea, boss."

"What about the rest of us?" Grayson asked.

"I think we should stake out Bricker and Stein's office," Bellamy commented.

I blinked, frowning his way. "Why?"

Bellamy crossed his arms over his massive chest, the t-shirt he wore pulling tight over the muscles. "I have a bad feeling that he's hiding something."

"We haven't spoken with his boss yet," Marv commented. "And I doubt he's used to dealing with situations like this."

Bellamy shook his head. "I didn't like the way he treated Harlow."

"It's fine," I said. "I know he's probably stressed and—"

"It's not that," Grayson interrupted as he looked to Bellamy. "He acts like that with most women."

"So he's misogynistic." I shrugged. "What does that have to do with the case?"

"Maybe nothing," Bellamy conceded. "But I'd still like to keep my eye on him. It couldn't hurt. If I don't find anything, then I don't find anything, but if I do…" He let the sentence trail off.

Marv nodded. "Okay, Grayson and I will go with you." He turned to Knix. "We'll call you if we find anything."

"Be careful," Knix warned. "We don't want to offend anyone at Bricker and Stein, especially not if we still need their cooperation in helping to find Jenna."

"Will do," Grayson agreed readily.

Knix turned to Texas. "I'd suggest you take a laptop with you when you watch for Ollison."

Texas scoffed. "As if I would be caught dead without one." Texas looked my way and winked. "Of course, Spider-Monkey is more interesting to me than any amount of code."

"Wow," I commented dryly. "How did I ever resist you?"

Texas jumped off the bed and stretched up on his toes, the hem of his shirt lifting to reveal a stretch of skin that drew my eye. "Don't know, Princess," he said. "I honestly don't know."

CHAPTER 11

I don't know what I expected a stakeout to entail, but for some reason, I thought it would be a lot more exciting. All of the cop movies and television shows I had watched made it seem like the people doing the stakeout were stationary for mere minutes—eating junk food and drinking crappy gas station coffee—before they were on the move. That wasn't the case.

We'd been watching Thomas Ollison's apartment building for nearly three hours when I cracked. "I can't take this anymore," I groaned. "There's nothing going on."

Texas glanced up from where he was typing away on his laptop in the driver's seat of the car Marv had gone out and rented for just this purpose. It hadn't occurred to me that any of them had international licenses considering that we hadn't really left the country before, but Texas had driven the thing over and parked it without an issue. I, on the other hand, was forbidden from driving it. Which didn't bother me because I still got turned around in trying to figure out why all of the cars were driving and turning in the opposite direction that I was used to. It felt weird to be sitting where the driver would usually sit but with no steering wheel before me. "It's a stakeout, Spider-Monkey, what did you expect?"

"I don't know," I admitted. "But I think it was something a little more hands-on than staring at a wall for three hours."

He chuckled, clicked a few things on the laptop and then closed the lid before sliding it down to the footboards. "We're not staring at a wall," he said.

"*You're* not," I complained. "You're staring at a computer screen."

"I can assure you, it's not any more interesting than what you're doing," he replied.

Crossing my arms over my chest, I slumped in the seat and glared out of the tinted windshield at the apartment building across the street. While there were multiple exits out of the building, due to the low brick wall around the property, there was only one entrance into the small courtyard that surrounded the complex.

"We've been here for hours," I complained. "Do we even know if he's going to show up? What if this guy's at work?" Almost as soon as the words had left my lips, a thought occurred to me. I sat up. "Wait," I said. "What does this guy do? Did we determine why he was picking Jenna up in the first place?"

"He's been in and out of employment for years, but from what I pulled up on his background, he seems to be working mostly menial labor jobs—all part time or contract based," Texas said. "Restaurant jobs, delivery jobs, those kinds of positions. He usually gets off around seven though, according to his timecards with his current employer."

"It's an hour past that now," I said, nodding to the digital clock on the dashboard.

Texas nodded. "Not everyone comes home straight away and considering the traffic in Sydney, he might not come back for several more hours. Knix didn't seem to think he'd be one of those come-straight-home types. It's likely we might not see him at all."

I returned to staring out the windshield at the gray brick building that was Thomas Ollison's home. "I just want this over with," I admitted. "I want to find Clarissa's niece and just know that she's okay."

Texas found my hand with his, reaching across the console and grasping my fingers in a firm, warm grip. "I know you do, Princess," he said. "We'll find her."

Though I wasn't convinced, I nodded anyway and sighed as we settled in to wait out the rest of our shift. Eventually, Texas pulled away and reopened his laptop while I kept my eyes glued on the complex. Every once in a while, however, I noticed him glancing at me out of the corner of his eye.

"Texas?"

He jerked his eyes back down to the laptop screen. "Hmmmmm?" he hummed innocently.

I shook my head. "What's up with you?" I asked.

"What do you mean?" he asked.

I pursed my lips and lifted a brow in his direction. "I'm not stupid," I said plainly. "You keep looking at me like you want to ask me something. What is it?"

Texas was quiet for a moment, unable to meet my eyes as he stared down at my hands in my lap. The silence stretched so long that I started to grow slightly uncomfortable. When I moved my hands from my lap to the sides of the leather car seat and curled my fingers around the edges, he finally took a breath and looked up, meeting my gaze.

Uncertainty settled in his expression. His mouth opened slightly, white teeth biting down on his lower lip as if whatever he was considering needed extensive thought before he just blurted it out. Seeing the reservation on his face unnerved me.

I turned towards him. "Hey." I reached for his hands and lifted them with mine. "You know you can tell me anything, right?" I asked.

He nodded. "Yeah, I know."

"Whatever it is, I'm not going to judge you," I assured him.

He released his lip and sighed. "I didn't think you'd judge me," he said. "It's not about—it's…just…"

Texas was normally so upbeat and expressive, it was like looking at a completely different person. His eyes were serious. His face drooped with solemnity rather than lifted with amusement. It was so out of character. My heart sped up. *Did he regret our relationship? The marriage? Was it the other guys?*

"I'm sorry," he said. "I'm fucking this up. It's not you. I don't want you to—" He stopped and took a breath as if steeling himself. "Bellamy told me that you didn't use a condom the last time you were together."

I blinked. Considering I'd had this conversation with

Marv only a few hours before, hearing Texas' words confused me. It hadn't been what I expected.

"I—I—" I had no clue what to say.

"You don't need to explain anything to me," Texas rushed to say, "but he was worried and he didn't know how to ask if you—if you're—"

"I'm on birth control," I said. "I didn't use a condom with Marv either."

"Oh." After a beat, Texas pulled his hands away.

Bereftness followed his action. "I didn't want to talk about it just yet, but we were going to talk to everyone when this was all over," I said.

"Birth control isn't one-hundred percent effective," Texas said quietly, his eyes lowering.

"I don't…" My breath struggled in my lungs, coming in short sporadic puffs of air. My body didn't feel like it was drawing enough in, and it was letting too much out. "Do you not want…?" I tried.

Texas' body clenched, but in the next breath, he slumped against the seat and bowed his head over his lap. Moving the laptop back to the floor, he set his elbows on his thighs and shoved both hands through his hair at the sides of his head. "A kid is a big deal, Harlow."

"I'm not pregnant," I pointed out.

"No, I know, but what if you were. You're going to want kids at some point. The guys might want kids. I wouldn't blame them and I could be that fun uncle, but…"

I shook my head, confused. "Texas, look at me," I said. For a moment, I thought he wasn't going to. He kept his face down, aimed at his knees. When he finally lifted his head, my heart broke at the expression on his face. "What's this really about?" I asked gently.

"What if it was mine?" he asked.

"A child?" He nodded and I released a breath. "Would that be a bad thing?"

"I don't know how to be a dad," he admitted.

The whole world narrowed to that statement. It was said with such certainty, and yet, such fear, that it made me realize why he was acting this way.

I slid across the seat and reached over the console to him. I rested my hand on his shoulder and smiled. "Texas," I began, "no one knows exactly how to be a dad, especially if they've never had kids before. You figure it out as you go along."

"My parents were shit, Harlow," he said. "They left, and while my grandparents were amazing, they weren't my mom and dad. How can someone who didn't have parents *be* a parent?"

"I think…" I bit my lip. "I think sometimes the people who didn't have parents can be the best at it." I recognized the emotion in his eyes now. It was fear. "No matter what happens," I continued. "I know you'd be an amazing dad."

"How can you be so sure?" he asked.

I leaned down and pressed my cheek to his, closing my eyes as I breathed in his scent. Somehow, he always smelled like sweet vanilla. I wanted to roll across him and lather myself in the fragrance of him. "I just know," I whispered against his skin. "I know because I know how much you care and what you're willing to do for your family. You would do nothing less than everything you possibly could for your kids." I brushed a kiss against his neck. "Trust me."

Texas didn't return my affection for several long moments. I simply stayed where I was, relaxed against his unyielding body until I felt the core of him soften and an arm come up, encircling my shoulders.

"I love you, Spider-Monkey," he said.

"I love you too," I replied. "I always will. Even if you're a bit dense."

He chuckled. "Me? Dense? I don't think so." His voice lifted as he looked up and stared out of the window.

"Oh, I definitely think so," I argued playfully.

"Harlow." Texas' arm left my shoulder and he sat forward. I drew away, startled by the abrupt change in his tone. His eyes were glued to something across the street. I stopped and followed his gaze, gasping when I saw what had captured his attention.

"That's him," I said, rushing to unlock the door.

"Wait." Texas' hand shot out and locked on the door handle as I moved to turn it. "Stay here, call Marv, and tell him that Ollison is back at his apartment first."

I nodded jerkily and reached into my pocket for my phone. I pressed the last called button and waited until the list of names came up. Clicking the green next to Marv's icon, I put the phone to my ear and stared out of the windshield as it began to ring.

"This is Marv. Sorry I couldn't get to your call, if you leave a—" I hung up and dialed Knix and then Bellamy and then Grayson, but received the same result each time. Shakily, I looked up at Texas.

"They're not answering." My voice trembled. One of them wouldn't have been cause for concern. Two would have been strange. But all four of them? They wouldn't have been unreachable without telling us something was going down.

"None of them?" Texas yanked his gaze from the complex and looked at the phone in my hand. I shook my head. He cursed low, snatching his laptop up and opening it with a snap. I looked over his shoulder, passing my attention back and forth between the building and what he was doing.

"Is that their phones?" I asked when he pulled up a map of the city and showed six blinking red dots. I assumed the two just outside the city were us since they were practically on top of each other. The four remaining dots, however, were inside the city. "They're together," I said.

"Yeah." Texas zoomed in. "They're at Bricker and Stein. All of them."

"Even Knix?" I asked as a droplet of rain slapped the windshield.

He nodded. "Their phones are still on. Everything looks normal."

"If their phones are on…" I gulped. "Why aren't they answering?"

"I don't know." Texas closed the laptop and reached into the backseat as more raindrops hit the top of the car and the side windows, sliding down the glass and blurring the image of the street outside. My eyes widened when I saw him lift out a case that I hadn't seen before. He opened it, revealing a small handgun.

"A gun? Are you even allowed to have gun in Australia?" I hissed.

"Marv got an import permit for it," Texas said as he leaned forward and tucked it into the back of his waistband.

"What are you expecting to happen?" The pitch of my voice shot up as he shrugged into a jacket.

"Hopefully nothing," he replied, "but I have to be prepared for everything."

I shook my head as he handed me a spare jacket that looked like it belonged to one of the guys. "I don't like this," I said as I shrugged into the coat.

"You don't have to come with me," he said, his brows drawing low. "It could be dangerous, I'm not sure you should—"

"You're deranged if you think I'm going to let you go in there alone," I snapped. "Do you know how many people with guns end up getting that same gun turned on them. If there are two of us, we have better odds."

"I think that's for home invasions," Texas said, shaking his head. "Don't worry, I probably won't even need to use it."

I reached for the door handle. "Let's hurry up and figure out what Ollison knows," I said. "The sooner we know, the sooner we can get to Bricker and Stein."

Texas nodded and reached for his own door handle. Releasing the locks, the two of us dashed out into the rain.

CHAPTER 12

Texas and I moved through the gate that led into the apartment complex's courtyard as rain fell heavy over our heads. I pulled up the hood on my borrowed jacket and stayed close behind. We approached the front door and found it unlocked. I could still hear the rain coming down as he stepped into the front hallway.

I sniffed as the smell of someone cooking drifted into my nostrils. "Do you know which apartment is his?" I asked as Texas strode through the first hallway, his head turning left and right as he scanned the apartment numbers, and since he never stopped, I could only assume they weren't what we were searching for.

He nodded. "He's apartment 204."

I moved to the side and started following the path of numbers. We reached the end of the hall and took a set of narrow stairs just large enough for us to go up single file onto the next floor. "204," I said, stopping in front of the first apartment I came across. We must have come up the back way.

Texas nudged me to the side and moved in front of me, raising his fist to knock. We waited a bit and when a gruff voice answered. "'Oo is it?"

"Mr. Ollison?" Texas inquired.

"Ye'?"

"My name is Texas Johnson; I'm here to take a statement on behalf of Bricker and Stein on the disappearance of Jenna Wiedleman."

"Disappearance?" The soft sound of locks being disengaged sounded immediately after that. Texas and I exchanged a look moments before the door cracked open and the rounded face of a middle-aged man appeared on the other side. "Jenna's missin'?"

I frowned. "You were the last one to see her, Mr. Ollison," I said, stepping closer into the alcove of his doorway. "You didn't know?"

He shook his head and then gestured for us to enter the apartment. "No, 'course I didn' know," he replied. "Please, why don' you come in? Would you like somethin' to drink?"

"No, thank you, Mr. Ollison," Texas said. "What can you tell us about the last time you saw Jenan Wiedleman?"

He wrung his hands. "Well, we met at *Bean Water*—s'near tha downtown stretch," he said. "She's a sweet girl, really. American, that one. Speakin' o', you have American accents, are you mates of hers?" He stopped and looked at us expectantly.

I nodded. "Yes, and we're very worried. We haven't seen or heard from her in a few days and she hasn't answered her phone or emails and she hasn't been to her apartment. Do you know where she could've gone?"

He grimaced and shook his head. "Last time I saw 'er, she needed a ride back to 'er office."

"You took her back to the office?" Texas demanded.

Startled by the sharp tone in his voice, the man nodded quickly, eyes growing wide. "'Course, didn' want 'er to waste 'er money on a cab," he answered.

Texas spun on his heel, reaching out and snatching my wrist as he tugged me behind him. "We have to go," he said.

"What? Why?" Texas didn't reply as he yanked me out of the apartment. Thomas Ollison stood in the doorway of his apartment, watching us as we retreated quickly. I sighed and called over my shoulder. "Thank you for the information, we appreciate it."

He lifted his hand in a half-hearted, confused wave. I would've returned the gesture had Texas not slammed through the door into the stairwell, nearly dragging me down the staircase as we went.

"Texas!" I tugged on my wrist. "Slow down, you're going to make me trip. Tell me what's going on."

Texas shook his head and refused to release me, but at least he began to speak. "It was never him," he said. "If he took her back to the office, then she's still there."

"What do you mean?" We pushed out into the apartment complex courtyard. The rain had begun to come down even harder as we rushed from the street to the car.

Texas hurried me to the passenger side door, made sure I was inside before he dashed around to the driver's side, and slammed himself in, shoving the keys into the ignition as lightning flashed across the sky and thunder rumbled.

"Stover—Bellamy said he didn't feel right about him and as we were waiting on Ollison to come home, I hacked into the security footage of *Bean Water* and was reviewing the time when Jenna would have left. I was trying to figure out why the images felt wrong. She was leaving, but—" he broke off and shook his head. "I can't believe I didn't see it."

"See it?" I lifted my brows and tilted my head as he turned the car around and headed back to downtown Sydney, back to the Bricker and Stein office building. "See what? Texas, you're not making sense. I'm confused."

"I thought it was odd we couldn't get anything on the businessman Bricker and Stein are prosecuting," Texas said. "He seemed too clean for a guy embezzling money. He doesn't live over his means, isn't spending money frivolously. I've checked his normal accounts. That's because he wasn't the man they were prosecuting."

"I'm sorry what?" I shook my head. "They're not prosecuting anyone for embezzling money?"

"No, they are," Texas assured me. "But didn't you think it was also a little odd that they'd send over a grunt worker like Jenna? She's just a paralegal. She does background work. But one of the reasons Alex wanted us to come check on her in person, is because Jenna used to work for Iris."

"She used to be an Iris girl?" Stunned didn't even cover what I was feeling. I was thoroughly confused and shocked.

"Yes." Texas took a corner a little sharper than expected and I nearly slid over into his seat. "Why aren't you wearing your seatbelt?" he snapped, his tone tinged with concern as he let up on the gas

"I'm getting it," I replied, my hand snapping out to grab at the rope of belt over my shoulder. We had been in such a rush that I'd completely forgotten.

Texas waited until I was securely buckled before he pressed his foot back on the gas. "She came over as a favor to her boss to do some digging. She was never prosecuting some random guy in another business."

"Then what was she doing?" I asked.

"She was looking for evidence to prosecute someone within Bricker and Stein."

My lips parted. "Stover…" The name echoed in the dim interior of the car as the rainstorm raged outside.

Texas tipped his jaw in a hard nod. "The guys must have figured it out," he said, cursing harshly. "I should've realized it sooner."

I reached over touching his arm even as he focused on the road. "It's not your fault," I said. "But do you think she found something—Jenna, I mean?"

"She must have," Texas replied. "Or he must have caught on."

"She can't be at the office, though," I said as he slowed at a light and turned my way with a frown. "He couldn't have kept her at the office or let us around so much if that was the case," I explained. "He certainly would have acted more nervous."

"I don't think you know men like him, Harlow," Texas said. "He doesn't care. If he's the embezzler, and if he's embezzling millions of dollars…you'd be surprised what men will do under the power of greed."

The light turned green and we sped forward. "Do you think he's going to hurt the guys?" I asked.

Texas' lips firmed into a straight line. "I don't know."

"How can he keep them there? It's four against one," I said.

"I guarantee you, he probably has people working with or for him. He's probably offered them a piece of the money pie if they'll help him get it."

I sank into the leather seat. My heart raced in my chest. The image of the guys being held at gunpoint flashed through my mind. My breath hitched and I chanced a glance at Texas. "Can you go any faster?"

He didn't respond, but I felt the car jolt as he pressed down harder on the gas. I watched the watery roads outside and swore that no matter what happened, we would make it in time.

CHAPTER 13

"Can you tell what floor they're on?"

Texas and I rushed into the lobby of the Bricker and Stein building, frowning when we saw that the front desk was deserted.

Texas pulled out his phone and clicked through a few apps, holding the phone out to show me a map of the interior of the building. It was in the same design as the building blueprints Knix often left lying around the house. I took the phone as we rushed through the elevators. I didn't know how he'd gotten the blueprints, but I didn't ask. With Texas' skills, it was often better not to know.

"Fourth floor," I said. "I think they're in the meeting room again."

He hit the button and we waited impatiently for the lift to rise. Texas reached back and slipped the gun out of the small of his back. I stared down at the phone screen. The red dots blinked bright and alive. And though I knew it was nothing more than a collection of cell phones with a signal connecting with the phone in my hand, I prayed that it meant the guys were okay. If they weren't…I didn't know what I would do.

"When the doors open," Texas said as he flicked the safety off on his gun, "we have to move fast. He'll hear it ding. If they are in the meeting room, I want you to let me go first."

"You said he might have people working for him, what if there are too many for you?" I asked nervously. "If they're too much for the guys then the two of us—"

"You let me worry about the guys," Texas said, keeping his eyes straight ahead, staring at the line that divided the elevator doors.

"Texas—" The ding of our arrival interrupted me and Texas moved forward, pushing me back as the doors slid open and he moved into the hallway with his arms raised and his gun pointed. Strangely enough, however, there was no one around.

We moved silently into the room, noting the darkened interior. "There's no one here," I said, staring down at the phone in my hand. "How—"

"The phones," Texas stopped at the end of the table and lifted one of the four phones that had been left behind.

"If their phones are here, but they're not…then where the hell are they?" Fear raced through my system. It clouded over my brain, making the whole room fuzzy. All of the air leaked out of my chest. If Stover did anything to my guys, I would make sure he would regret it. No matter what I had to do. No matter what rules or laws I had to break.

I strode over to Texas and handed him back his phone. I looked at him pointedly. "Find them," I ordered.

Texas met my stare for a moment before he turned the phone his way. His fingers flew over the screen as I collected the rest of the phones and we made our way back out into the hallway. I led him into the elevator and back down to the lobby. We strode out of the building and went back to where we'd left the car running on the corner. I didn't even feel the rain as it splattered the side of my face and soaked my hair, making the strands stick to my cheek.

Texas got behind the driver's seat and tossed the phone in my lap as he cranked the car. "Laptop" he snapped, holding his hand out. I reached beneath the seat and retrieved it.

I glanced down to the phone screen as he clicked open the computer and let his fingers span across the keyboard. I lifted the cell in a shaky grip. It was security footage of the guys as they were led with their hands behind their backs out of the Bricker and Stein building. Every single one of them carried stiff shoulders and stony faces.

"His fucking house!" Texas growled, practically throwing the computer into my lap as he punched in something on the car's GPS system.

"You found them?" I demanded.

"He took them to his fucking house," Texas answered. He pressed the green start button on the screen and turned the wheel, steering onto the street. "I can't believe it. He's so stupid. I didn't think anyone would be stupid enough to take hostages to their own house."

I reached up and buckled in, my hands clenching on the seat as we fishtailed taking a turn too fast. The only way I was going to keep a level head was to keep Texas talking. It distracted me from my surroundings. "Why would he take them to his house?"

Texas shook his head, his focus centered between the road and the GPS. "It's not his actual house," he said. "It's a property he owns—a small vineyard outside of the city."

"How'd you figure that out?" My knuckles turned white as he ran a red light.

"CCTV," was all he answered.

I squeezed my eyes shut. "Texas, they're going to be alright."

"I know that."

"We'll get to them in time."

He jerked a firm nod.

"Texas?" He flicked me a sharp look—one so unlike him that it unnerved me. "Just don't kill us before we get there."

Fire danced behind his eyes, the fury in his expression was only growing more and more alarming. I reached over and took the gun from where he had set it in the console. I checked to make sure the safety was still off and then I gave him a meaningful look.

"You'd be really mad if you died before you could kick someone's ass."

He followed that with a snort and another slight tilt of his head. "Okay." He took a breath and let up on the gas. Texas' normally soulful brown eyes burned like embers in a dark fire. And if Stover hurt my guys, I would unleash that fire. I'd make sure he burned in it.

Vineyards smelled of grapes, I realized. Fruit and flowers. The scent surrounded us as we crept through the rows and rows of grapes. I felt suffocated by all of the smells. It was so heavy in the air that I held a hand over my mouth and nose as we moved towards the house at the top of the hill.

As we approached the back veranda, a swinging sign that read *Little Hill Vineyard* caught my attention. A golden glow of lights illuminated from within. Texas and I trailed up to the back door and when we found it locked, he handed me the gun and bent down to check it out. After a moment he withdrew a small ring of keys from his pocket. I frowned at them as he slid one partially into the lock, glanced my way, and smacked his hand down hard turning the key at the same time.

The door popped open. "How...?" I whispered as I handed him back the gun and he slipped the ring of keys back in his pocket.

"Bump keys," he said quietly before putting a finger to his lips and gestured for me to step to the side.

We entered through a kitchen, the sound of voices drifting down from somewhere above. We both looked up as we heard a distinctive shout and a crash. "Stover," I said, moving towards the stairwell.

"Harlow, no," Texas hissed, but it was too late, I was already halfway up the stairs. I paused, turned, and gestured for him to follow. "I should go first," he said, moving past me. "Stay behind me and if any of them have guns, I want you to run."

"Fat chance," I whispered.

"What?" He turned and looked back at me.

"You got it," I lied. There was no way in hell.

He narrowed his eyes at me. "I mean it."

I nodded and nudged him forward. "Let's go."

Texas turned and lifted the gun in his hand as we crept up the stairwell. My heart raced against my ribcage, pounding so loud that I swore it was as if the damn organ was hooked up to a speaker. I could hear it in my ears.

"—tell me where the evidence is and you can all go home," I heard Stover saying as we neared the second floor. Texas paused and put his hand back to keep me from continuing forward as we listened to the response.

"Where do you fucking think it is, you idiot?" I bit my lip at Grayson's remark. There was a beat of silence before a sharp thump and a responding groan.

"I've been incredibly patient with you, Jenna," Stover continued, "but this is your fault. You got these people involved—"

"You got them involved," I heard a feminine voice—assumedly Jenna—interrupt. As Texas and I moved closer to the corner, and I leaned past him to peek around the corner, I spotted them through an open doorway into what looked like an office. I was right. It was her. "If you hadn't embezzled hundreds of thousands of dollars, none of this would be happening."

"It was three million, you little bitch," Stover snapped with a growl. "A million dollars. Do you know how much it costs to even live in Sydney? I left my life behind in Texas to come here and what do they repay me with? They wanted me out! I took what I was due."

There was a deep rumble as a man encased in all black —black cargo pants, black shirt, and a black mask covering his whole head—strode by the doorway and said something. I looked to Texas, but it appeared that neither of us could make out whatever was being said by the man.

"They're *what?*" Stover screeched. "Get them in here now!"

Texas moved down a step, pushing me back as the man in black appeared in the doorway once more, this time heading in our direction. "Go," Texas hissed, motioning for me to retreat back down the stairs, but as we turned another man in the same attire—all black everything—appeared at the end of the staircase, effectively trapping us between them.

I could see indecision cross over Texas' face and then he quickly lifted the gun and took aim. I gasped as the gun went off and covered my ears as they began to ring immediately after. The man at the top collapsed, clutching his leg as he groaned. Texas swung around and pointed the gun at the man from below.

"I wouldn't if I were you," Texas warned as he backed up the stairs, pulling me with him. The man watched us through the eye holes in his mask. It was hard to tell from his expression, but from the tension in his body language, he wasn't happy. We moved past the fallen man as he rolled and clutched at his leg, cursing a blue streak so rapidly that it became all gibberish to me. Texas swung around as Stover appeared in the doorway. "Harlow, get the others," Texas commanded.

I rushed ahead, moving past Stover with as minimal contact as I could. He scowled at Texas, keeping his eyes trained on him even as a bead of sweat rolled down his forehead.

"Harlow, what—you shouldn't—" I rushed to Grayson's side as he struggled to move away from the wall.

"Don't worry about that now," I said, as I shoved him forward and frowned. Reaching into his pockets, I felt it when he stiffened as I brushed against something that was *not* what I was looking for. "Are you serious?" I said as I found the pocket knife he kept and used it to slice through the zip ties at his wrists.

He shrugged. "Can you really blame me, Doll?" he asked with a rueful grin. "You're here. The blood is pumping. Texas is holding a gun…" There was a pause. "Why the fuck does Texas have a gun?"

I moved to Marv and cut his restraints next. "It was for emergencies," Knix said with a sigh as I got to him.

"And this counts as an emergency," I replied.

I cut through everyone's zip ties, ending with Jenna who looked a little worse for wear. Her hair was matted against one side of her head, and dark circles lined the creases beneath her eyes. "Thank you," she muttered when her restraints were finally off. Everyone rubbed at their wrists as they slowly got up from the floor.

Knix took control and moved behind Stover as Texas trained the gun on him. Texas had moved to the side to keep the other men in his sight the entire time. I tossed Marv one of the cells I had kept and he quickly dialed.

"We need to get out of here," Jenna said.

"I'm calling the authorities," Marv said. "You may still get to see him in court, but there's no doubt Stover is going to prison."

Hearing him, Stover rounded on the room. "I deserved that money!" he screamed. "They were—where are you going?" He turned again as he spotted the two men in black, one helping the fallen one up as they slipped down the staircase.

Texas moved to follow them. "Let them go," Knix barked, making him freeze and turn back. "We just want Stover for now. We can get them later."

"No," Stover backed up, away from both of them. His eyes wide and wild. He shook his head from side to side. "No, I don't—No!"

"Stover, don't be stupid," Grayson warned as he put his hands out and circled the man.

But he was going to be. I could see it. He was beyond help. Overexertion had made him shiny with sweat. His gaze darted around, never landing on one thing or one person long enough. And then they settled on me.

"Stover, don't do anything stupid," Bellamy warned, moving closer to me as Jenna backed up, her brow puckering. She knew something was up. Stover was losing it far too quickly.

The man was shaking so hard, I could practically hear the rattle of his bones. My body ached from how tight my muscles were coiled. The world slowed down to a frame by frame set of images as I watched Stover reach behind him. One of his hands going to the desk he had backed himself into.

My head lifted at the same time that he swung the gun my way. His lips tried to shape words, but I couldn't hear anything. The rushing in my ears made it too loud to hear anything. It all narrowed down to the barrel of the small pistol Stover pointed at me.

His gaze was unfocused, his face red as his finger pressed against the trigger. In the distance, I heard shouting. Bellamy was the closest to me. Out of my periphery, I saw him dive, aiming for me. The bullet slammed into me a split second before Bellamy did, trying to cover my body with his own. The air was knocked from my chest.

I blinked as I collapsed. My eyes were open, but I couldn't feel the pain yet. My whole body didn't seem to be working. My limbs were immovable and though I tried to focus on where I was hit, tried to feel where the bullet had entered, I still couldn't feel or hear anything.

A flurry of movement erupted past me. Bellamy's face appeared above me as he ripped his shirt off and pressed it against my stomach. Of course, Stover wouldn't miss. Even as shaky as he'd been, it would have been hard to not miss with how close we were.

I opened my mouth, but no words came out. My eyes trailed down the hard lines of Bellamy's chest. He was beautiful. Even when his eyes were full of terror. Marv's head came over me as well. A phone pressed to his ear once more as he tried to ask me something.

I shook my head. I couldn't hear him. The room was fuzzy, the edges of my vision blurring out and growing dark. *Shouldn't it hurt?* I wondered. Getting shot was supposed to hurt.

"Harlow?" The sound of my name made its way into my brain and I cracked my lids open. When had I closed them? "Stay with me, stay with us. Help's on the way."

My tongue felt swollen in my mouth. My eyes slid shut on their own accord and this time, they didn't open again.

EPILOGUE

1 year later...
Texas

My fingers tapped impatiently on the hardwood of the sitting room side table. I bit the inside of my cheek as three of us waited for Harlow, Knix, and Marv to return. Across from me, Grayson shifted his right leg over his left, changing it for the tenth time. To my side, Bellamy flipped a page of the magazine he was pretending to read.

I almost made a comment. I knew he wasn't reading it. For one, it was upside down, and for another thing, it was a women's health magazine and his eyes had this glazed over look that he sometimes got when I tried to explain the process of hacking into a government database or something along those same lines.

None of us were as put together as we would have liked the others to believe. My heart pounded in my chest, beating a rapid thump that didn't seem to be slowing down no matter how many times I took a deep breath and released it.

"Stop worrying," Grayson finally said, glaring at where my fingers tapped out the tempo of my heartbeat on the side table.

I lifted a brow and smirked. "I'm not the one acting like he has to pee but doesn't want to ask where the bathroom is," I replied.

He shook his head at me and went back to his phone. I went back to tapping.

Minutes later, the door opened and Harlow appeared in her sundress, a bright smile on her face as she held the hand of a little girl with the darkest corkscrew curls and the biggest brown eyes. As soon as she saw us, she backed up and hid halfway behind Harlow's skirt. I damn near stopped breathing. She was so cute. Sweat broke out on my forehead as Bellamy and Grayson stood and moved forward.

"Guys, this is Delise," Harlow introduced, putting a gentle hand on the young girl's shoulder.

Knix and Marv came up from behind her and Delise moved closer to our girl as they passed her. "She'll be staying with us from now on." Harlow looked down at the girl. "Honey, do you want to say hello? That's Bellamy"—she gestured to Bell—"and Grayson"—she gestured again—"and that"—Harlow stopped and winked my way—"is the naughtiest one of all. That's Texas."

I stared at the little girl as I approached and crouched down as slowly as I could manage. "Hi, Delise," I choked out.

I held out a hand, wondering if what people said was

true. Could kids really tell if a person was good? As I watched, staring into Delise's eyes—the same color as my own—I wondered if things had gone differently if we would be in the same place we were now.

I still had nightmares. I glanced up as Harlow smiled down at me. I knew she did too. For as long as I lived, I would never forget the sound of Stover's gun going off. Seeing the blood soaking through Harlow's clothes. Hearing her hit the floor. Having to face the line of doctors weeks following the event even as Stover was tried for embezzlement and attempted murder.

Knix stopped at Harlow's other side, one wide palm going to her stomach as he leaned down and pressed a kiss to her forehead. I felt like an ass, worrying as I had about the possibility of her getting pregnant. She never would now—the bullet had done too much damage.

A small hand touched mine. I slowly returned my gaze to Delise. She inched out from behind Harlow, settling her small grip firmly in mine. "Hi…"

I gulped. "Do you like games?" I asked.

She stepped slightly closer and nodded. I reached into my back pocket and pulled out my cell phone. Clicking the screen on, I flipped through to a few of the apps I'd created and clicked on one, turning the screen her way. "Do you see this?" I asked, pointing at the monkey on the screen. "His name is Bruno. You have to help him get through the maze because he's lost and needs to get home."

"Home?" Delise asked.

I nodded, swallowing roughly as I gave the phone over to her completely and stood up. Her little face glowed with wonder as she tapped the buttons on the screen and moved the character around.

"Let's go get the car, Delise," Marv suggested, holding out his hand.

Distractedly, the young girl moved closer to him, reaching up with one tiny palm to latch onto his much larger one. Together, they headed for the door, leaving me to stare after them.

"What do you think?" Harlow's voice was quiet, hesitant.

I looked back at her. I couldn't do anything but admit the truth. "She's beautiful," I said.

Harlow smiled. "And now she's ours." I nodded. Knix glanced between the two of us. As if he sensed that I needed to say something, he backed away and followed the rest outside. "You're still scared," Harlow said as soon as he was gone.

I released a slow breath. "I don't think I'll ever not be scared," I admitted.

She moved forward and leaned up on her toes to kiss me. Warmth infused every inch of the connection. I closed my eyes and reached up, holding her by her arms as I returned the kiss, pushing her mouth open and diving inside. My tongue met hers. I felt her eyelashes flutter against my skin.

"I love you," I whispered as I broke away a moment later.

"I love you too," she replied. "And I think you're going to be a great dad. You all will be."

"I can't believe they let us do this," I said, pulling her in so that I could wrap my arms around her.

"With the six of us, how could they not?" she asked. "Nothing can stop us if we're together."

I shook my head, a laugh rumbling up. "My grandparents would have loved you," I couldn't help but say.

She chuckled against my chest, pressing another kiss to the hollow of my throat. "I think I would have loved them too, if only because they raised you into one of the men I could never live without."

I held her close for a moment more, wanting to extend the feeling of her in my arms. Even if I knew I could do this whenever I wanted—even though she was my wife—I would never tire of the sensation of holding her.

Letting her go was like letting go of a piece of my heart. After watching that piece nearly be destroyed by a money hungry idiot with a grudge a year ago—watching her struggle to get back to who she had been and fight to overcome the doctors telling her she'd never have kids—I wanted to give her everything. Even when I wanted to lock her away, I knew she needed freedom. She needed a choice.

And to give her that, I needed to overcome my fears. I needed to see the world as she saw it because I didn't want her for a moment in time. I wanted her forever and always.

The End.
For realz this time.
Thank you so much for reading.

ABOUT THE AUTHOR

Lucy Smoke, also known as Lucinda Dark for her fantasy novels, has a master's degree in English and is a self-proclaimed creative chihuahua. She enjoys feeding her wanderlust, cover addiction, as well as her face, and truly hopes people will stop giving her bath bombs as gifts. Bath's get cold too fast and it's just not as wonderful as the commercials make it out to be when the tub isn't a jacuzzi.

When she's not on a never-ending quest to find the perfect milkshake, she lives and works in the southern United States with her beloved fur-baby, Hiro, and her family and friends.

Want to be kept up to date? Think about joining the author's group or signing up for their newsletter below.

Facebook Group
Newsletter

ALSO BY LUCY SMOKE

Fantasy Series:

Barbie: The Vampire Hunter Series
Rest in Pieces
Dead Girl Walking (Coming Dec. 2019)
Ashes to Ashes (Coming early 2020)

Dark Maji Series
Fortune Favors the Cruel
Blessed Be the Wicked
Twisted is the Crown
For King and Corruption (Coming Soon)

Nerys Newblood Series
Daimon
Necrosis
Resurrection (Coming Soon)

Dystopian Series:

Sky Cities Series
Heart of Tartarus
Shadow of Deception
Sword of Damage
Dogs of War (Coming Soon)

Contemporary Series:

Iris Boys Series (completed)
Now or Never
Power & Choice
Leap of Faith
Cross my Heart

The *Break* Series (completed)
Study Break
Tough Break
Spring Break
Break Series Collection

Standalones:

Expressionate
Wildest Dreams

Manufactured by Amazon.ca
Bolton, ON